SPITFIRE

D1048323

Bobbie hadn't enjoyed having to sell her home to the forceful Rod Simpson—but she had to admit that he had been very kind and tactful about it, even to the extent of letting her go on living there. It was all quite respectable too, as long as his sister was living with them—but what happened when she got married and went away?

SPITFIRE

BY

LINDSAY ARMSTRONG

MILLS & BOON LIMITED
15–16 BROOK'S MEWS
LONDON W1A 1DR

First published 1981
Australian copyright 1981
Philippine copyright 1981
This edition 1981

© Lindsay Armstrong 1981

ISBN 0 263 73611 3

Set in Monophoto Times 10 on 12 pt.

Made and printed in Great Britain by Richard Clay (The Chaucer Press) Ltd, Bungay, Suffolk

CHAPTER ONE

ROBERTA HALLAM sank down on to a dusty bank beside the road and gave way to an emotion she didn't often indulge in. She burst into tears.

The tears surprised her almost as much as they surprised her dog Bluey, and he thrust his cold nose into her face and tried to lick them away.

'Oh, Bluey,' she sobbed, and hugged him to her, 'what am I going to do now?'

Bluey responded with a shrill bark and wriggled in her arms in an ecstasy of affection.

'That's all very well,' she told him between sobs, 'but it doesn't help me to conjure up a tyre. And until I can figure that out, I'm well and truly stuck. I'll miss the race!'

She raised her head and surveyed the battered, dusty horse-float attached to her equally battered, ancient car which now stood at a curious angle because of one very flat tyre. And if that wasn't bad enough, the spare tyre lay in the road and bore mute testimony to a similar condition.

'Why didn't I check the spare tyre?' she asked herself despairingly. She rubbed her eyes with her knuckles and in the process transferred most of the dirt off her fingers to her face, but still the tears flowed. And she realised suddenly that she was not only crying out of frustration but for all the crushing events that had overtaken her young life in the past several months. She was crying now as she had not been able to when her parents had been killed in a car smash, and she had been left with a small farm and eight trotting horses to manage single-handed. Crying now for the pile of debts that seemed to be rising daily. Crying for the race that she was going to miss—the race that she was so sure she could win and the prize money which would have solved so many of her problems. Crying because at eighteen her secure, happy life had suddenly become one long nightmare.

It was Bluey who brought her back to the present with a start. His body stiffened beneath her hands and a low growl rumbled in his throat. He jerked himself out of arms and started to bark. Roberta raised her head wearily and noted with surprise that the hair down his back was standing straight up and he was growling again deep in his throat and showing his teeth in a savage snarl.

Her gaze followed Bluey's outraged stare and came to rest on a pair of very expensive, elegant leather shoes planted beside the float in the dusty road and flashed upwards, and with a startled exclamation she scrambled to her feet.

Bluey barked again, and the owner of the brown shoes unfolded his arms from across his chest and said with a faint tinge of mockery in his voice, 'A damsel in distress, I see. For a moment I thought you were a boy.'

'But I didn't. . . .' She looked around wildly and her eyes fell on a low-slung silver-grey sports car parked ahead of her own car. 'I didn't hear you,' she said lamely. And then with a stirring of hope in her heart. 'I've got a flat tyre. . . .'

'So I see.' White teeth glinted in a tanned face and a pair of amused grey eyes beneath a well-tended thatch of thick brown hair rested briefly on her face and then travelled slowly down, taking in her crumpled jeans and jacket. She couldn't resist a sudden feeling of embarrassment at her dishevelled state and put her hands up to her hot face.

'Don't,' he said lazily. 'You can only make it worse.'

She gritted her teeth as the embarrassment seeped away rather quickly and a feeling of annoyance took its place. Her green eyes took on a defiant sparkle and she tossed her head with its cap of dark red curls. It was all very well to stand there and laugh at her, she thought furiously. And then, as her eyes took in the tall figure in well-cut cream linen trousers and the brown silk shirt he wore under a beige sweater, a doubtful expression crossed her face. How could she ask this man to help her change a tyre?

He grinned again as if he was able to read her mind and then turned to survey the car and float. 'What beats me,' he murmured, 'is how you got this far.' He gestured towards the gig which was hooked on to the back of the float. 'I take it you're heading for Kilmore trots?'

'Yes.' She stepped forward hesitantly. 'Do you ... would you happen to have a spare tyre I could borrow? I know it sounds crazy, but I could give you my address. I live in the district and I could change it myself. You wouldn't have to get yourself messed up. But you see I've got a horse in the third race and I've simply got to get there....' Her voice trailed off helplessly and she was conscious that his glance had sharpened as it rested on her face.

'Tell you what,' he said after a moment, 'I've got a better idea. I've got a tow bar on my car. I think we should unhitch your float and put it on my car. At least you'll be assured of arriving in one piece that way.'

She stared at him. 'Do you mean . . . leave my car here?'

'Yes.'

'What if someone pinches it?'

He burst out laughing and shook his head. 'Take a brave person to pinch it! Well? What do you reckon?' He looked at a gold watch with a brown alligator skin band on his wrist. 'As it is we'll only just make it.'

Roberta said agitatedly, 'It's very kind of you, but I've still got to get home, you see.'

'I'll take you home. You said you lived in the district, didn't you? And then perhaps you could get your spare tyre repaired and retrieve your . . . er . . . car at your leisure?'

'Well——' She twisted her hands in an agony of indecision and at that moment the patient horse in the float, patient up to now anyway, gave a very impatient whinny. 'All right,' she said hurriedly. 'Thank you very much. I'll get the horse off so we can change over. Please don't get yourself in a mess, though. If you could manoeuvre you car round, I can do the rest.'

'I don't doubt it,' he said with that tinge of mockery again. 'But I'm not in the habit of standing around and letting a slip of a girl heave and strain. You just worry about the horse, I'll do the rest.'

And true to his word and with very little effort, he effected the changeover and they were on the road with Bluey in the back seat and looking unusually subdued and almost humanly puzzled at the change in circumstances.

Roberta glanced at her rescuer obliquely as she sank back into the well-upholstered seat and the powerful motor under the long, sleek bonnet roared to life. And looked away quickly as his glance intercepted hers. She'd been thinking that his elegant image hid a powerful body and the thought had caused a strange sensation at the pit of her stomach.

Her eyes jerked back to his face as he said, 'I think this calls for some introductions, don't you?'

'Oh yes!' she said apologetically. 'I'm Bobbie Hallam. And I really can't thank you enough for what you're doing.'

'Bobbie?' His eyebrows rose enquiringly.

'Roberta, actually,' she explained. 'I think my parents were rather set on having a son, you see. They'd even picked out a name—Robert. That's how I came to be called Roberta. Which is an awful mouthful, you must admit, and ever since I can remember I've been called Bobbie.'

'Bobbie,' he said again, and laughed. 'Have your parents got over their disappointment, or are you still trying to live up to their expectations of a son? I must say you almost look the part.' His grey eyes roamed over her again.

She frowned and said stiffly, 'I look this way because it's the most practical way to dress for the life I live. When you're messing about with horses all the time, it's silly to get all togged up.' She glanced contemptuously at his own immaculate clothes. 'But I don't expect you to understand that. I should imagine the most you've ever towed with this car is a . . . fancy boat or something like that. And for your information, my parents were marvellous people and I loved them very much!' She stuck her chin out aggressively and her eyes sparkled furiously at him.

'Wow!' He ducked playfully. 'Remind me not to

cross swords with you again, Miss Bobbie Hallam,' he chuckled, and then his face sobered at her look of injured dignity. He took one of his strong brown hands off the steering wheel and put it lightly on her knee. 'I'm sorry, it wasn't a very nice thing to say. You talked about your parents in the past tense?'

'They're dead,' she said flatly.

'Oh.' He didn't say anything for a time as he concentrated on passing a large cattle truck. And then, 'This horse you're taking to Kilmore—who's driving it for you?'

'I'm driving it,' she said defiantly. 'I've got a licence—now, and what's more I'm hoping to win on it. If we get there in time, that is.'

'Is that a fact?' he drawled, and his eyes had an added glint of interest as he took them off the road for a brief moment and surveyed her. He put his foot down and the car jerked forward. 'Well, we'd better get moving, hadn't we? Tell me, how long have you had a licence?'

Bobbie clutched at the armrest as the car spurted forward and the countryside flashed past at a dizzying speed. 'Um ... this is my first drive at a registered meeting, but I've been driving for years. Are ... do you ... aren't we going awfully fast?'

'Not if we want to get there in time for your first drive,' he said, and added with an unkind laugh, she though, 'But if I had any sense I'd settle down to a crawl.'

'Why?' she demanded angrily. 'I'm perfectly capable of steering a horse around! I've driven at shows and trials.'

'Bobbie. . . .' he began, then heaved a sigh. 'Never mind, it's your business. I wish you well on your horse.'

'Thank you,' she said proudly. 'And you're right, it *is* my business.' And she shut her mouth firmly, determined not to engage in any further conversation.

But as they turned into the float entrance of the Kilmore track a niggling thought caused her to say lamely, 'There's just one problem.'

He raised his eyebrows at her.

'It's Bluey,' she said. 'I shouldn't have brought him really, but he gets lonely at home.'

'So? You can tie him up in the float, can't you?' he said as he steered the car into a space between two trucks.

'He hates being tied up in the float. He barks and wails and makes a terrible fuss. But. . . .'

'Don't tell me. He'd be all right in the car.' He switched the engine off and turned to her. 'O.K., he can stay. But I warn you, if he chews anything or does anything else unacceptable, he'll be one very sorry dog!'

Bobbie settled the strap of her helmet more comfortably under her chin and pulled her goggles down. She wished the palms of her hands weren't quite so sweaty as they grasped the reins. And a maxim of her father's flashed across her mind. Anything you feel, he'd always said, you transmit to your horse, even when you're sitting behind it in a gig. They can sense indecision from the touch on the reins.

She took a deep breath and resolutely turned the mare Best Dressed towards the starting tapes. And as they paced along the wide Kilmore track she said soothingly, 'Come along, old Bessie. I know it's not your regular driver in the gig, but you're going to do your best for me, old girl, aren't you?

To which stricture Bessie replied with a flicker of her ears and a swish of her tail.

Besides, Bobbie added to herself, with a swift glance towards the fence where the crowd was already gathering, there's someone out there who obviously doesn't think you should be doing this. So let's just show him what we can do!

And with a small spurt of surprise she realised that she had not discovered her rescuer's name. She frowned momentarily at something stirring beneath the surface of her mind. In the agitation of paying for Best Dressed and getting the mare harnessed up and herself changed into her colours and white trousers, she hadn't paid him much attention. As a matter of fact, after helping her in with the horse and gig and harness trunk he had disappeared and only reappeared just before she had gone into the marshalling yard. But something else struck her as they jogged along. He had seemed well known to the throng of trotting people around the horse stalls—very well known, if one could judge by the exchange of greetings that had rung out. Who was he? she asked herself. And why had he stood and looked at her and the mare so assessingly just before they went into the ring, as if he had wanted to tell her something? She pondered, but was unable to come up with anything.

A gig and horse ranged up beside her. 'Good day, Bobbie!' the driver called across. 'See you got your licence. Good on yer, mate!'

Bobbie smiled at the figure in the orange and green silks. 'Thanks, Ted,' she called back. Ted Wilson had been a friend of her father's.

'How's your horse going?' he asked confidentially as they pulled their horses up.

'All right, Ted. I think I've got a fair chance. She seems to be back to her best form.'

He gestured towards Best Dressed. 'She's no slouch when she's right, Bobbie. Don't get caught in the death, though, and watch out for Number Six. It's down from New South Wales and the word's out it's a flying machine—if it steps.'

She looked around. 'Who's got it?'

'Chris Williams is driving it today, but. . . .'

The rest of his words were drowned out as the starter called the field up. Best Dressed was drawn Number Four and Bobbie lined her up on the front line. She stood quietly enough, but Number Six, a bold flashy chestnut, was playing up and delaying the start. Bobbie felt her nerves tighten as Best Dressed stirred and started to sweat.

And then the starter dropped his arm and the tapes flew back and the field surged forward. Out of the corner of her eye Bobbie noticed that Number Six galloped for a few strides, but Best Dressed was pacing beautifully and she got to the lead easily and settled her on the fence.

The smooth brown track sang as it flowed beneath the wheels of her gig, and it was the only sound apart from the thudding of hooves and creaking of gigs she could hear as they paced down the back straight. Round the bend and down the front straight they flew, and Bobbie was conscious of the murmur of the crowd as the winning post loomed up and a bell rang to signify that the last lap was coming up.

She took a look over her shoulder and was surprised to see the flashy chestnut behind her in the death seat. It must have found its gait immediately after galloping and lost very little ground. She sneaked another look round, to see it was gaining on her, inch by inch.

All right, don't panic, she told herself. Just sit tight!

And she sat tight until they entered the back straight. But the chestnut horse was now level with Best Dressed and his driver was easing his whip out of the gig, and Bobbie was thrown into an immediate dilemna. She'd hoped to make her move on Best Dressed a little later. The mare had a short sharp sprint for about four hundred metres. Anything much over that generally found her wanting. And this was too far from home.

She cast another desperate look across at the chestnut horse and saw the driver raise his arm with the whip in it.

On the other the hand, she told herself as she switched both reins to one hand and drew her whip, it was now or never!

She tapped Best Dressed up and the mare responded gamely and surged ahead. And as soon as she turned back and saw the chestnut horse drop off, she knew she'd been had.

Chris Williams had forced her to go too early and he was now giving his own horse a breather. But having set Bessie alight Bobbie knew it was no good hauling her in and then trying to get her to sprint again. She wasn't a horse that could stop and start, and the only thing to do now was let her sprint and hope.

Bobbie set her teeth and took the mare round the last bend and into the home straight. And her heart went out to Bessie as she used the whip and moved desperately in the gig seat as the winning post drew closer and the roar of the crowd filled her ears. It was as if she knew just how much was riding on this race, plus an innate distaste for being beaten, which kept the mare going, but Bobbie knew she was beaten halfway down the straight as that chestnut nose ranged up alongside her, gaining ground with every stride. Then another horse loomed outside of it and the winning post flashed by on the inside of her, but several metres too late.

The chestnut horse had won the race and Best Dressed had been beaten into third place.

Chris Williams pulled his goggles down and saluted her as they pulled their horses up and turned them around.

'That was a great drive, Bobbie! And you've got the old mare going real well.'

'Thanks, Chris.' She wiped her forehead wearily and another of her father's maxims came to her. There's nothing worse than a sore loser, he had always said. If you're beaten fair and square take it with a smile and wait until you get on your own before you gnash your teeth.

She grinned across at Chris. 'I shouldn't have fallen for that old trick! But that's a good horse you've got. To gallop and sit in the death and still win—some horse!'

'Yeah. Wish he was my own. But you know, Bobbie, it ain't that easy to drive in the lead. There's always some joker willing to take you on or kid you anyway. You just ask around and you'll find plenty of older, more experienced drivers'll tell you how many races they've lost like that. But your dad would have been proud of you, the way you drove the mare out.'

'Thanks, Chris,' she said again, and lined Bess up in third spot against the fence.

The officiating steward checked her whip and winked at her. He was also an old friend of her father's.

He said, 'I can see you're just a chip off the old block, Bobbie! Keep it up, lass, you'll be on the winning list shortly.' And he raised him arm to signal the all-clear.

I won't think, Bobbie told herself tiredly as she steered the horse back towards the stalls. Not till I get home, anyway. Because there is just no way I *can* keep going now.

She was still holding tight to her emotions as she walked the mare around to cool her down. She glanced over her shoulder to see if there was a wash bay free yet and led Bess towards one just being vacated.

But how can I leave all this? she asked herself as she tied the lead to the chain on the wall and reached for the hose. She looked around at the colourful throng of people, some of whom she had known all her life, at the horses now parading for the fourth race, and her heart sank in her breast like a stone.

It was as she turned the hose off that she became aware of the conversation in the next wash bay. She couldn't see who was in it, but as she took up the iron scraper she recognised the voices and stood poised with the scraper in her hands.

It was Chris Williams, who said quite audibly, 'It was like taking lollies from a baby. I can tell you, I didn't feel too good about it.'

But it was the voice that answered him that caused her to start and drop the scraper. 'It's a tough game, Chris. If she can't take it she shouldn't be in it.'

'Oh, she took it all right, like a proper old stager. But still. . . .'

And that voice again almost impatiently, 'How's the horse pulled up, Chris? He's nominated for Moonee Valley on Saturday and I want to run him.'

'Real good. . . .' But Chris's next words were drowned by the sound of water running and Bobbie was in a sudden fever to get away before they realised she was there.

Because Chris's words had brought home the real truth to her. She had lost the race like a proper novice despite his earlier kind comments. And that other voice which belonged to the owner of the chestnut horse, belonged to the man who had rescued her from the roadside. The man who had laughed at her and never once mentioned that he had a horse in the same race.

Oh, I could die, she told herself as she raced Bess out of the wash bay and back to the stall. And one thing's for sure, I'm not going home with him even if I have to ride Bess all the way. What a sucker they must take me for!

She looked around despairingly as she tied Bess up and her eyes fell on Ted Wilson, and without giving herself time to think it out she dashed across to him.

'Ted? Ted, have you got room for another horse in your truck? And me?'

'Bobbie! Ted turned to her in surprise. 'Sure I have, love, but what about your own float?'

She explained about her car. 'I'll leave my float here overnight, Ted. It should be safe enough. And tomorrow I'll get it all sorted out.'

'How about the person who towed you in?'

'He . . . he's going in the opposite direction. I don't like to ask him. . . .' she said mendaciously, and added anxiously, 'Is it a lot of bother for you, Ted?'

'Of course it isn't, Bobbie. Tell you what, we'll stop by your car on the way home. I've got a few tyres in the truck and we might be able to get it going. Only one thing, love, I was planning to leave pretty soon. . . .'

'That's suits me fine, Ted. Just give me ten minutes and I'll meet you at the truck.' And she dashed off.

Back at the silver-grey sports car, she wriggled her slender wrist through the narrow opening in the back window which they had left open to give Bluey some air and with some contortions she managed to unlock the door from the inside and release the excited dog.

'Down, Bluey!' she commanded. 'I've got to write a note quickly, mate. Let's see. . . .' She chewed the end of her pen reflectively for a second and then dashed off— Thanks for the lift. I'm going home with friends. I'll leave the float here overnight and collect it tomorrow— and signed it with a flourish.

Now all I've got to do is unhook the float, she told herself, and I can get away from this place and hopefully never lay eyes on you again, Mr Who ever-you-are! She placed the note prominently on the dashboard and relocked the car carefully. She turned to the float, then clenched her fists in exasperation.

The wheel-prop that supported the float level when it was unattached and had a winding mechanism on it to facilitate the unhitching was securely locked in the boot of the car.

'Bother!' she said out aloud, and Bluey barked in agreement. 'I don't think I could get it off without the prop. It's too heavy,' she told him confidentially, and he blinked wisely at her and lolled out his pink tongue.

'Well, I'll just have to leave it on. He can take it off. It'll serve him right for being such a. . . .'

Bluey barked helpfully.

'Yes, that's just the word I wanted,' she told him. 'Come on, old son, let's get out of here!'

And she was just drifting off to sleep much later that night after doing the endless chores and resolutely refusing to allow herself to think of the future, when she was struck by a sudden thought.

She sat upright and Bluey moved protestingly at the end of the bed. 'Surely he wouldn't pinch my float?' she asked the sleepy dog. 'No.' She sank back to Bluey's relief. 'No, he wouldn't to that. It's far too shabby for him!' Bluey didn't reply, but thumped his tail once.

CHAPTER TWO

THE Victorian weather did one of its surprising turnabouts during the night and Bobbie discovered as she went about her early morning chores that from early autumn yesterday, it was today chilly winter.

When she had the last horse worked and put back in its box, she walked slowly up to the house, blowing on her cold hands. The day was bright enough, but a sharp, cold wind was blowing the long, dusty grass in the paddocks and rattling through the gum trees that surrounded the house.

Bobbie paused on the doorstep and looked back the way she had come. The farm, as her parents had fondly called it, was really a smallholding of about twenty-five acres. But oh, such dear acres, she thought as her eyes skimmed the small trotting track and moved up the gentle slope of the hill beyond. The paddocks were beginning to turn brown now and the dam in a corner, between a fold of the hill and the track and stable area, was going down very slowly. They needed rain.

Her eyes swept up to the top of the hill again and a huge, solitary tree that stood on the crest. From up there one could see around the countryside for miles—as far as Kilmore, in fact, which was fifteen miles away. She breathed deeply and with an abrupt movement turned and went inside with Bluey on her heels.

She stoked up the old-fashioned woodburning stove that her parents had kept in the kitchen for warmth and put the coffee pot on.

She breathed deeply again and looked around the warm, cheerful room with its glow of burnished copper that her mother had lovingly collected over the years and its bright red curtains and windowboxes. The house had originally been an old stone barn which her father had converted. There were three bedrooms upstairs, but the downstairs area had never been completed and it was still one large room that served as kitchen, lounge and dining room. But it had an old-fashioned charm, with chintz-covered chairs, plump and comfortable and a great old oak table that her father had unearthed at an auction sale and restored.

No, she thought suddenly, I still can't bear to think of leaving it all. And she took the rolled-up newspaper the mail man had delivered earlier and poured herself a cup of coffee.

She unrolled the paper as she sat down at the table and opened it from long habit at the sports page. The results from the Kilmore meeting were on the second last page and as usual there was a small column devoted to the meeting. Half way down the column there was a picture of a driver complete with helmet, and she frowned for a moment. Rod Simpson, the caption said. Well, Rod Simpson was almost a household name in the trotting world. He had been the leading driver in New South Wales for some years, but she couldn't fathom what he had to do with the Kilmore meeting. She stared at the face under the helmet and wondered who he reminded her of. Of course, faces under helmets always looked a bit different, she mused, and moved her eyes back to the beginning of the article.

So that was it, she thought as she read. Rod Simpson had moved his establishment to Victoria . . . she started as she read on. In fact the would almost be her next-door neighbour!

'Well, what do you think of that, Bluey?' she asked out aloud. 'The rich and famous are moving into the old Turner place. Things are looking up, old son!'

The sound of a car outside distracted her and she rose from the table and moved across to the front windows—and gasped.

For there in her driveway, just drawing to a halt, was that familiar silver-grey sports car and attached to it and, even more familiar, her own horse float.

Her heart raced suddenly and she stood rooted to the spot, unable to think clearly. What on earth could she say to the man? How dared he do this to her? she thought not very coherently, and jumped as the door knocker sounded loudly.

Bluey responded immediately by barking shrilly and she saw through the lace curtain that the man outside had turned and was looking thoughtfully at the rear end of her car as it poked out of the garage beside the house.

I can't even pretend I'm not here, Bobbie thought wildly.

Bluey barked again.

'All right, all right, I'm coming!' she muttered to him, and gave him a quelling look. She opened the heavy wooden door and said lamely, 'Good day.'

He had his arm raised to repeat his knock. He dropped it and thrust his hand into his pocket and surveyed her for a moment without speaking.

She quailed inwardly at the cold look in his grey eyes and swallowed. She could think of absolutely nothing to say.

'Good day to you, Miss Bobbie Hallam. As you see, I've returned your float. I'm surprised you weren't worried that I'd pinch it.'

Colour flooded her cheeks. She said stiffly, 'Thank you for bringing it back. It wasn't necessary, though—I was going to pick it up myself this morning.'

'Oh, were you? He crossed his arms over his chest and stood looking at her.

She fumed at his assessing look, for she was in an even worse state this morning than she had been yesterday. She straightened her shoulders and glared back at him.

He laughed softly at her, but his eyes were still cold and mocking as he said, 'Tell me, Miss Hallam, what did I do yesterday to deserve the kind of treatment you meted out? Surely it would have been only common courtesy to come and find me at the trots and let me know you'd made other arrangements to get home? I spent some time searching for you, you know, before I went to the car and found the note.'

'I'm sorry,' she said abruptly, and her pent-up emotions took command before she quite knew what she was about. 'If you really want to know,' she said hotly. 'I resented the fact that you didn't tell me you had a horse in the race, and I resented your and Chris Williams' inferences that I wasn't fit to be driving. But at least Chris had the grace to feel a bit uncomfortable about his statement—taking lollies from babies! Whereas you no doubt found it only a cause for mirth. No!' She raised a hand as he started to speak. 'This isn't sour grapes, as you probably think. I admit quite freely I was tricked out of the race and I'm not complaining about that. It's all part of the game, and I also

admit that your horse would most likely have beaten
Best Dressed anyhow. What I do object to is your atti-
tude. I told you free, gratis and for nothing that I had a
horse in the race and I hoped to win. But you told me
nothing, and then you had the nerve to sneer at me
afterwards. Are you surprised I never wanted to see you
again?'

His eyes had narrowed thoughtfully as she spoke. He
said, 'So it was you in the next wash bay. Don't you
know eavesdroppers never hear good of themselves?'

'I . . .' she spluttered, 'I wasn't eavesdropping! I
couldn't help but hear what you said. . . .'

'Nevertheless you missed the whole point,' he said
tersely, 'and I don't intend to explain it to you out here
in this perishing wind. Or is this yet another example of
your discourtesy?'

She said through her teeth, 'I consider your actions
yesterday a vast discourtesy. Much greater than mine
and. . . .'

But she didn't finish her statement, because with a
look of blazing anger in his eyes he grabbed her by the
shoulders, thrust her inside and bundled her into a chair
at the table.

She shot up with a look of disbelief in her eyes and
opened her mouth to call to Bluey, but her mouth
dropped open limply as he forced her back into the
chair with a heavy hand on her shoulder and at the
same time commanded Bluey to sit.

Bluey sat and grinned at them both foolishly and
thumped his tail on the floor.

Bobbie caught her breath. 'How dare you!' Her eyes
blazed at the man and she switched her gaze to the dog.
Bluey uttered a shrill bark but didn't rise.

The hand left her shoulder. 'I wouldn't depend too much on your dog, Miss Hallam.' His white teeth flashed in an amused grin and he pulled out a chair for himself. The grin faded and he said deliberately, 'Now you're going to listen to what I've got to say whether you like it or not. I didn't tell you about my horse yesterday quite deliberately, because I didn't want to sap your confidence. It's difficult enough to go out on a track for your first drive without having the knowledge that you'll most likely be beaten. And after all, I didn't know your horse or its ability, and you did come pretty close to winning the race. With an ounce of luck you would have won.'

She glared at him and said contemptuously, 'You don't believe that for one minute! You don't even believe I should be driving. Although what *you* know it about I can't imagine. Wealthy owners are very critical, but you get out there on a track with a horse, if you could bear to dirty your hands, and see for yourself, and then you can come and gloat to me about taking lollies from babies!'

He shot her a surprised look.

She closed her eyes briefly and then said with a small sigh, 'Look, I admit I'm only a novice and I fell for the oldest trick in the book. You and Chris were quite right in that respect, but I felt . . . I just felt you . . . could have at least told me you had a horse in the race. I didn't expect you tell me how good it was or anything like that. I know that wasn't any of my business, but . . . and then afterwards the thought of you and Chris laughing about me—well, it was just too much.'

He said nothing for a moment but looked at her steadily. Then, 'Bobbie, we weren't laughing at you.

You drove that horse as well as most other people.' He gestured towards the open newspaper. 'If you read that article you'll see you even get a mention in it. What Chris meant when he said those unfortunate words, and he only explained it to me afterwards, was that he knew you were in some sort of financial straits and he would have dearly loved for you to win the race. And my own words—I know they must have sounded harsh to you, but they still hold true—racing's a business and no one can afford to allow sentiment to enter it. Which was why he won the race the best way he knew how. He did nothing illegal.'

She refused to meet his eyes. 'I'm not blaming him at all,' she said in a small voice. 'If I'd had any sense I'd have engaged the best driver I could find.' Her glance rested on the open paper and the picture of Rod Simpson and she said with an attempt at a wry grin, 'If only I'd known he was going to be there yesterday. . . .'

Her voice trailed away and her eyes widened. There was no sound in the room but the ticking of the clock as she raised her head slowly and looked across the table incredulously.

Her voice sounded hoarse to her own ears as she said helplessly, 'You . . . why . . .! Oh, why didn't you tell me?' She scrambled up and with her hands to her hot cheeks turned her back to him and walked over to the stove. She stared unseeingly out of the back window and tried desperately to recall exactly what she'd said to him: 'What you know about it, I can't imagine . . . all you've ever towed is a fancy boat!' She closed her eyes in horror. This, to Rod Simpson who some hailed as the best driver in the country. Who was known in all states for his cool and daring. Who had the best horse in the country in his stable . . . and who was going to be her next-door neighbour, almost.

Oh, heavens, she thought, I wish the floor would just open up and swallow me!

But the floor remained obstinately closed beneath her feet and she felt his hand on her shoulder again, although this time more gently. He put his finger beneath her chin and forced her to look up at him.

'I guess this sounds rather egotistical, but I assumed you knew.' He grinned at her. 'At least by now, anyway,' he added with a whimsical quirk to his lips.

Bobbie flushed again, burningly conscious of all things of his fingers on her chin and desperately surprised by this.

He dropped his hand and said lightly, 'Why don't you offer me a cup of coffee, Bobbie? Perhaps we could go back to square one now and start off on a better footing.'

She could never afterwards actually recall making the coffee, but finally she was sitting down opposite him with two cups on the table between them and desperately trying to think of something to say.

He took the dilemma out of her hands. He looked around and said, 'I like your house. It has an atmosphere. As a matter of fact I was coming to see you about something else today, a business propostion I'd thought of before I made your acquaintance yesterday.' He chuckled at the look of surprise on her face. 'You see, it so happens I've come down here a month earlier than I'd planned. I . . . er . . . incurred the stewards' displeasure in Sydney last week and received a month's suspension for my pains. They took a dim view of me pushing out through what they described as the eye of a needle, in a race, but as a matter fact I could have got a semi-trailer through if necessary—however, that's by the way.'

'That's . . . that's why you weren't driving yesterday?' she ventured.

'Quite. Anyhow, it seemed senseless to sit in Sydney and twiddle my thumbs for a month. Now, my horses are arriving in a couple of days' time, but the stabling on this property I bought from Ken Turner isn't finished yet and won't be, I've now discovered, for a good two months. So I was wondering if I could rent some boxes from you. Someone has told me that you have about six spare ones, and I was also wondering if I could rent the use of your track until I get myself sorted out.'

She looked at him wonderingly. 'Would you . . . plan to stable Morningtown here!'

'Sure. And about five others. And the rest of them I'm putting out to spell.'

Morningtown. Bobbie traced a pattern on the oak table with one finger. Some called the brown stallion a freak horse. Indeed, some of his feats had been freakish. She remembered her father saying that he would be happy to have a horse with just a quarter of Morningtown's ability. To be able just to see a horse like that working on her own track every morning. . . .

'I'm very sorry,' she said quietly, 'it's not possible. You see, I've virtually sold the place, to a pig breeder. He'll be taking possession in about ten days' time.' There, it was out at last. She'd spoken those dreaded words, admitted to herself finally what must be done. A curious calm numbness stole over and she raised her eyes to his probing ones.

'Bobbie,' he said finally, 'would you like to tell me about it?'

'There's not much to say.' Her voice was flat. 'Chris was right when he told you I was in financial straits. The bank have been very kind, even to the extent of finding a prospective buyer so I can sell the place privately. But the terms of the sale are that they have almost immediate possession on a renting basis until the deal is finalised. I . . . was hoping yesterday to win on Best Dressed, which would have given me the money to catch up with the mortgage repayments, but really it would only have . . . prolonged the issue. I . . . I'm going into town this morning to sign. . . .'

She jumped as he banged the table with his fist.

'How come your parents left you in these straits?' he demanded. 'Surely a seventeen-year-old kid deserves something better!'

She sprang immediately to their defence. She said angrily, 'They didn't plan to get killed! Everything was all right while Dad was alive. He planned to invest in some new horses, which was why he took out the extra mortgage. We'd had a couple of lean years, so we didn't have much cash to throw around. But it was a joint decision—I mean, he consulted me and my mother about it. And I supported it! It was the sensible thing to do. The only thing that's gone wrong is that I'm . . . not as good as he was. And for your information, I'm eighteen!'

'Okay,' he said coldly, 'but these unaccountable accidents do take place, and a wise person takes that into account.'

'Don't,' she jumped up and stood over him, 'don't you criticise my father! And he hasn't left me . . . destitute. Once the mortgage is repaid there'll be some left over. And I'm strong and healthy. I can get myself a job.'

'Sure. And walk out and leave all this behind you. All those years of effort for what? So that someone can walk in and start breeding pigs.' He stood up.

Bobbie steadied herself with an effort. 'I think you'd better go, Mr Simpson,' she said pointedly. 'I don't think we can achieve anything by discussing this further. You're probably only upset because you're in an awkward situation now. . . .'

She gasped in fright as he towered over her with a murderous look on his face. He said through gritted teeth, 'Someone should take you over their knee and spank you, Bobbie Hallam—you little spitfire!'

'Just you try it,' she said furiously. 'I'd fight you tooth and nail!'

He laughed suddenly and seemed to relax. 'You could try,' he murmured. 'I doubt if you'd have much success, though. For instance, Miss Eighteen-year-old, what would you do if I decided to treat you like a girl, instead of a scrubby tomboy—like this?'

He drew her into his arms. She stood rooted to the spot, her face a study of frozen incredulity as he tilted her head back and she was staring into those mocking grey eyes. 'And this,' he drawled, and lowered his head, and she felt his lips upon her own.

Every muscle she possessed seemed to be paralysed except her heart, and its rate suddenly trebled at one stroke. And for a brief instant she was aware of two things only. His lips upon her own and the hard strength of his body pressed aginst her.

And then he was holding her at arm's length and laughing softly at her. 'Did you say eighteen?' he asked wryly. 'You could have fooled me.'

He released her, and as a crowning insult, patted Bluey on the head and let himself out of the front door, while she stood stock still as he had left her but with one hand raised to her lips and a dazed look in her eyes.

Bobbie sat up on her bed where she had taken refuge to indulge, for the second time in as many days, in a storm of tears. But these tears were somewhat different. They were an expression of rage and frustration and directed at one person.

Rod Simpson. She clenched her fists and a renewed wave of hot colour rose from the base of her throat and stole across her cheeks. Why had she allowed herself to simply stand there like some limp rag? Why hadn't she fought him tooth and nail as she'd threatened?

She looked around at the little room, at the flowered wallpaper and the matching Dolly Varden dressing table and bedspread. It was a girl's room, complete with a Raggedy-Ann doll her mother had made her when she was a toddler.

With an impatient movement she slid off the bed and stared at herself in the mirror. And the face that looked back at her seemed to be somehow—unfamiliar. But why? she asked herself. The dark red hair and green eyes were the same, so was the pale skin and faintest dusting of freckles and the delicate column of her throat. It must be something inside of me, she thought, something I don't quite understand because it's never happened to me before. My whole life has been filled with horses, horses, horses. Until today. But now it's as if something inside is struggling to get out.

And show that insufferably conceited man; she closed her eyes—yes, that was it! Show him she wasn't a scrubby tomboy. And while I'm on the subject, also

show him that I'm quite capable of 'being in the game',
quite capable of running a stable and driving trotters
even against the likes of him. She stuck her chin out—
and there she was forced to pause.

'Oh, Bluey!' She sat down on the bed and pulled him
on to her lap and fondled his ears. 'You weren't much
help to me today, old son, were you?'

Bluey wriggled cautiously and tried to lick her face.

'Never mind,' she said, 'I forgive you. He must have
that effect on everyone. Maybe that's why he's so successful. Bluey, there's no help for it, I'm afraid. I have to
go . . . and see the bank today. There's just no sense in
putting it off.' She hugged the dog and hid her face in
his soft fur for a moment. Then she straightened and
pushed him off her lap resolutely. 'Tell you what,
Bluey,' she said with a tremor in her voice, 'we'll have
lunch first. I'm starving! How about you? Breakfast
seems like an awful long time ago. Hey, boy!'

And Bluey thumped his tail energetically.

Bobbie stared across the desk at the bank manager.
'Say that again, Mr Prentice,' she said breathlessly. 'I
don't understand. . . .'

'It's quite simple, Bobbie,' he said kindly. And you
know if . . . you must know if there was any way out of
this, I'd be the first one to rejoice. Unfortunately there's
not, but this offer will leave you with more cash, it's a
definite offer and it would be criminal of me not to
persuade you to accept it.'

'But . . . but when did you get it? Last time I spoke to
you, and it was only a few days ago, you said nothing
about it.'

'I didn't know then. It came . . . more recently. But

there's no doubt that the prospective buyer is quite genuine.'

A sudden suspicion crossed her mind. 'Who is it?' she demanded. 'And what do they want the place for?'

'It's a company.' He glanced down at the papers in his hands. 'Moreton Holdings. And they're not obliged to divulge the use to which they intend to put the property. Moreover, it's a cash offer and the terms of possesion have been left open pending discussions between yourself and the purchaser ... er ... Moreton Holdings, as I said. They gave me to understand that you would have more time in which to arrange other matters, for example the sale of your horses.'

She flinched perceptibly. Mr Prentice removed his glasses. 'Bobbie, I know how you feel. I've known you nearly all your life, and I know just what a wrench this is going to be. But as a business man and your bank manager I must advise you to accept this offer. You see, with the extra cash you could open a savings account and together with the interest and possibly other savings you may make, one day in the not too distant future it wouldn't be inconceivable for you to find another, smaller piece of ground, perhaps, and start another—operation on a smaller, more practical scale.'

'It isn't . . . it isn't someone called Simpson, is it?'

He replaced his glasses. 'Do you mean Rod Simpson? I believe he's just bought the Turner place!'

'Yes, of course,' she said, and coloured. 'Very well, Mr Prentice. Show me where I sign.'

CHAPTER THREE

BOBBIE put the last feed-bin in place and closed the paddock gate behind her. She had turned the four horses she had in work out this morning because it was pointless, not to mention expensive, to keep up a work program.

She stood with one foot resting on the gate and stared over the paddock. Bess was being her usual bossy self and moving from each of the four bins in turn with her ears laid back and attempting to chase the three other horses away. Typical Bess, Bobbie thought wryly, then turned away with a heavy sigh. The weather had deteriorated if anything and she shivered inside her plaid coat

'Well, there's nothing more I can do out here, Bluey,' she said. She looked at the man's watch on her slender wrist. 'I suppose we should go up and make ourselves ready for the representative of Moreton Holdings. According to Mr Prentice,' she told Bluey, 'he'll be here at eleven o'clock.'

It was warm and cosy inside and she had a late breakfast and tidied up and then went upstairs to change. She stood in front of her wardrobe and pondered. It wasn't an extensive wardrobe by any means, but at her mother's insistence it wasn't entirely made up of jeans and slacks. Her mother had been the most feminine woman Bobbie had ever known and her father had sometimes twitted her about how different she was. But her mother had always come to her defence. 'She's got years ahead of her, Bert. Don't rush her—I think she'll surprise us one day!' she had always said.

Bobbie smiled mistily, and whether it was out of fond memory of her beloved mother or whether it was because she was conscious of a need to present a more dignified or older image, she couldn't decide, but she drew a soft tweed skirt out of the wardrobe and a fine cashmere jumper that matched her eyes almost exactly and returned the slacks she had laid out earlier.

Bluey thumped his tail approvingly.

'That's all very well, Bluey,' she told him, 'but I'm not sure if I've got any tights—oh yes.' She pulled a packet out of a drawer. 'Now for shoes.' She delved among the shoes at the bottom of the wardrobe and came out with an elegant pair of brown leather court shoes with a medium heel. She looked at them doubtfully for a moment. They were brand new, in the sense that she had never worn them but they had been there in the wardrobe for several months. In fact they were the last thing her mother had bought her.

She stirred. 'Oh well, Bluey, I'll give them a go,' and Bluey grinned at her.

She stared at her reflection in the mirror when she was dressed finally, and pulled a face. 'If it's painting the lily you're after, Bobbie Hallam,' she told herself, 'I don't think you've achieved much,' and added, 'What you need is some make-up.'

Her fingers hovered over her mother's make-up kit which lay in the drawer, but at the sound of a car downstairs she slammed the drawer shut and pulled a comb hastily through her hair.

'It'll have to do, Bluey,' she said. 'Anyway, I don't really know why I'm going to all this trouble!'

A middle-aged gentleman with horn-rimmed spectacles stood before her on the doorstep.

'Miss Hallam? How do you do? I'm Geoffrey Goddard and I'm a solicitor representing Moreton Holdings.

'How do you do?' Bobbie murmured. 'Won't you come in? I think it's getting colder if anything.'

Geoffrey Goddard looked around him appreciatively. 'Charming,' he said. 'Quite charming.' He sat down in an armchair.

'Thank you. I'm . . . I must admit I'll be rather sorry to leave it,' she said, and thought at the same time, what an understatement!

'Well, as to that, Miss Hallam, there's no immediate necessity for you to do so.'

She jumped and stared at him.

He went on, 'On behalf of my clients, I've been instructed to advise you that they do not seek complete possession of the property for some time.'

'How . . . how long?'

'Let's say an indefinite period at the moment, Miss Hallam. Er . . . Mr Prentice has put us in possession of certain facts relating to your . . . er . . . circumstances. I must say he did this in your best interests, Miss Hallam, and my clients, once aware of these circumstances, have come up with a proposition. They would like to offer you free board in the house for a period which you could determine mutually, and a small salary in return for your services.'

She wetted her lips and looked at him in utter bewilderment. 'What services?' she stammered.

'Your services as strapper.'

'A strapper? So they've got horses?'

'Yes, indeed.' He beamed at her. 'Mr Prentice led me to believe you would prefer the thought of horses to pigs. I must say I can't blame you.'

She said dazedly, 'But I don't understand. Do they want to live here too?'

'For a period, yes. I believe it's a very common practice to engage a live-in strapper.'

'Well, yes, it is. The hours one works with horses make it very practical. I. . . .'

She stopped and stared at him. She had been going to say that she didn't think she would appreciate being a boarder and an employee in her own home, but something held her back. Wasn't it a false sense of pride? she asked herself. Wouldn't it be better than moving to Melbourne and trying to find a job? Surely anything would be preferable to that.

She said lamely, 'But they don't know me. They might not like me. And I thought it was a company.'

'A family company,' he said. 'And they've taken the liberty of seeking character references, and if I may say so, everyone in the district speaks most highly of you.'

Bobbie blushed.

He added, 'Of course, until the sale is finalised, and that's been set in hand this morning, but it will take some weeks, they will pay you rent. Would you like time to think about this, Miss Hallam?'

'I . . . don't . . . know,' she said disjointedly.

'If you're wondering about their characters, Miss Hallam, I can vouch for them personally, and also put you in touch with several professional men who would be only too happy to do the same.'

Her gaze fell on Bluey sitting quietly at her feet.

'I'll do it,' she said suddenly and resolutely. 'When do I meet the family, Mr Goddard?'

'If you could be home this afternoon about five they would be most happy to call on you.'

She was struck by a sudden thought. 'What about my horses?'

'I think you could arrange that this afternoon, perhaps? I have no instructions in that regard.'

When the solicitor had departed Bobbie sat for some time in a brown study with her chin in her hands trying to analyse her feelings. Finally she rose with a shrug.

'We can only give it a try, Bluey,' she said, but somehow it seemed as if the weight around her heart had lifted just a little.

It was Ted Wilson who brought that weight crashing down again. She telephoned him to tell him that she had left his tyre at the garage and had her own repaired. The garage proprietor, a friend of hers and Ted's, had promised to deliver it to Ted some time today with a truck part he was taking out to him.

'That's fine, Bobbie,' Ted said heartily into the phone. 'Congratulations, by the way. You'll be the envy of the district, lass. If you had to lose the place, this is the best way it could happen. Any kid would give their eye teeth to be in your position now.'

'What . . . what do you mean, Ted?'

There was a slight pause, then Ted said, 'Don't tell me I got it all wrong, Bobbie? Rod Simpson's bought your place, hasn't he? And he wants you to stay on. Old Billy Williams was telling me in the pub last night.'

'I think you have, Ted. I've sold the place to a company called Moreton Holdings. Simpson's bought the Turner place.'

'But that is Simpson, Bobbie,' Ted objected. 'I know because he's got a stud farm out west and I've bought a few yearlings off him. It's his family company. Bobbie? Are you still there, Bobbie?'

'Yes, I'm here,' she said through stiff lips. 'But I've got to run, Ted. See you!' And she dropped the phone down as if it was a hot cake.

How . . . oh, how could she have been so naïve? Her first suspicions had been correct then. But Mr Prentice . . . had he been in on the conspiracy too?

She discovered she was shaking with rage.

'Oh no,' she said aloud through her teeth. This was one battle Mr Mighty Simpson was not going to win. And to have the nerve to want to share the house with her! Of all the. . . . She picked up a small bowl on the telephone table and hurled it across the room.

Bluey looked at her reproachfully, but she ignored his look and picked up the phone again.

'West Vic Carriers? Oh, good, this is Bobbie Hallam of Greentree Farm. I've got some horses to shift. . . .'

Bobbie glanced at her watch. It was four-thirty. She had to be hitting the road or else she would run into him. She glanced down at the note in her hand. It read: Dear Mr Simpson, I've changed my mind since I spoke to your solicitor this morning and have decided to make a clean break from this property. Accordingly I've arranged for my horses to be picked up tomorrow morning and have already fed them for the night. I've shifted all my gear and gig to one corner of the tack-room and will make further arrangements to have it collected as well as the furniture in the house. I hope I haven't overlooked anything, but in that event, I will be forwarding you my solicitor's address in the near future. Signed, Bobbie Hallam.

I should have put Roberta, she thought, and I forgot to mention the float. Well, it will just have to do. She put the note down in the centre of the oak table and weighted it with a small vase.

'Come, Bluey!' she called, and without a backward glance she shepherded the surprised dog into her heavily laden car.

'Now don't you play up on me,' she said sternly to the car and Bluey, 'because I've got to get away from here fast. And don't you start to cry, Bobbie Hallam,' she told herself. 'Take a deep breath and drive away.'

A light, chilly mist swirled around the dark countryside adding an unpleasant dampness to the cold air.

Bobbie looked at the luminous dial of her watch. Nine o'clock. She'd been in this spot on this little-used country road for over three hours. Perhaps I should try again, she thought, and accordingly she switched on the motor and pumped energetically with her foot.

But the engine didn't even turn over. She sighed despondently as Bluey snuggled up to her. She had planned to spend the night at a motel on the outskirts of Melbourne and had been looking forward to a hot bath and a good meal. Planned, that was, until the engine in the old car had coughed and shuddered and mysteriously died. And stayed obstinately dead despite all her efforts.

I shouldn't have spent so much time with the Edwards, she told herself. And I shouldn't have taken this cross-country route instead of the highway. She thought longingly of the stove at home, but shook her head almost immediately. No good thinking backwards now. There was only one way to go, and that was forward. She yawned suddenly and realised she was desperately tired. All the packing and moving around she'd done that afternoon had taken its toll.

'There's nothing else to do, Bluey, so we might as well have a nap.' She had toyed with the idea earlier of walking back to the nearest homestead, but that was several miles away and she didn't like to leave the car, and all her possessions particularly, on the road.

'Somebody's bound to come along some time,' she told the dog.

And indeed someone did finally come along. She didn't hear the car come up because she was in a half doze, but the screech of tyres as it pulled to a juddering halt in front of her roused her suddenly, and she flung open her door and scrambled out into the damp, misty night. She could see a tall figure in the glow of the other car's lamps, advancing towards her, but she couldn't make out the person's features.

Then a curious thing happened. Bluey brushed past her, barking happily, and flung himself up at the tall figure in a joyous welcome. Bobbie stopped and stared, then took two steps backward as the figure advanced towards her. It couldn't be, she told herself stupidly. Her eyes flew to the car. It was. The yellow and black New South Wales plates were dimly lit but unmistakable.

Some instinct which she couldn't control caused her to turn and run into the mist. But he overhauled her in a few strides and grabbed her arm and held it in a firm, painful grip.

'Let . . . let go off me!' she panted, and struggled desperately.

'Are you crazy?' he demanded furiously, and swept her up into his arms.

She kicked and squirmed without making the slightest impression on him and finally found herself deposited in the front seat of his car. He slammed the door on her with a menacing look, then walked swiftly round to the driver's side and got in himself. He switched off the headlights and reached up for the interior light and turned to her.

'It's going to give me some pleasure to teach you a few lessons before you get much older, Bobbie Hallam,' he said roughly. 'And for starters you can explain to me why you flung my very generous offer in my teeth. Don't you want to stay at Greentree Farm? Don't you want to work with horses? Forgive me for saying so, but I got the obviously mistaken impression that *that* was all you wanted out of life. Perhaps you could tell me where I went wrong?'

She took a deep breath. 'I don't want your . . . charity!' she spat at him. 'I'm quite capable of looking after myself, thank you!'

'So I see,' he commented dryly. 'That's why you've allowed yourself to become stranded on this deserted road, easy prey for anyone who came along.'

'Like you,' she said contemptuously. 'You tricked me into selling the farm to you with your fancy price and then you had the nerve to expect me to live in the same house as you. What did you expect? That I'd fall into your arms—out of gratitude? Well, you can think again!'

To her surprise he threw back his head and laughed, then said with a glance that seemed to strip her naked, 'I may have some faults, but cradle-snatching isn't one of them.'

'Oh!' She lunged at him, intent on she knew not what as a rich tide of colour suffused her cheeks. But he caught her wrists in one lean, strong hand, in a biting grip.

'That's enough,' he said brusquely. 'I'm going to tell you a few facts of life, and if you have any respect for your own safety, you'll keep your mouth shut while I do. It was no fancy price I paid for your property. It was a fair and equitable price that would have come your way eventually had you been in a position to wait for it. Unfortunately it's fairly common knowledge that you were in dire straits, and the pig-breeder's offer was geared accordingly. And your bank manager did the right thing when he advised you to sell. Despite being a family friend, he had his hands tied on account of the mortgage.'

Bobbie stirred, but the grasp on her wrists didn't relax and she subsided as he continued relentlessly.

'However, it goes against the grain with me to see a good horse property, that's been lovingly built up, handed over to a bunch of pigs. Particularly when it suited my purposes to acquire it, just in case you should think I was acting out of pure altruism.' He let go of her wrists. 'Perhaps you have something to say now?'

She swallowed and licked her lips, massaging her wrists. 'But you've only just bought the Turner property. Why. . . .'

'And I've also been negotiating for the property between the Turner place and Greentree Farm. However, the Meads aren't anxious to sell, but since buying your place I've been able to negotiate an easement through their place which links the two properties and I now have fifty acres all in all, which is about what I wanted.

I still haven't decided which one I'll live on finally, but in the meantime, your set-up will do.'

'I see,' she said in a small voice. 'But why all the secrecy? Why didn't you come out and tell me this in the first place?'

'If you recall our last meeting, Bobbie,' he said wryly, 'you'll remember that we didn't part on the best of terms. And I didn't have much faith in, let's say, your maturity, to think you'd allow yourself to make a rational decision. And it seems I was right.'

'That was your fault!' she shot at him angrily.

'Well, perhaps,' he conceded lazily with an amused look in his grey eyes that infuriated her.

'Besides,' she said hotly, 'it's impossible for us to live alone ... I mean, in the same house. Heaven knows what people would think!' She added stiffly, 'So if you could see your way clear to give me a tow to the nearest garage, I'd be very grateful. It's ... best for me to carry on, on my way as I decided.'

'Where to?' he asked with lifted eyebrows.

'I ... well, I'm not sure yet. But,' she added spiritedly, 'I'll think of something!'

Rod Simpson said nothing for a moment, but his face sobered and then he said almost gently, 'I'm sure you would, Bobbie. As it happens I am going to give you a tow, but straight back home again.'

She started violently and opened her mouth to protest vigorously, but he waved her to silence.

'To a hot bath and a meal and bed, in that order.' His grey eyes roamed over her, taking in the grease smears on hands and cheeks and her dishevelled clothes. 'You look desperately in need of all three,' he drawled, 'and to set your mind at rest, I have no intention of moving in with you until my sister arrives, which she should do in a couple of days, and then she'll live with us too. So you can forget all the desperate visions of seduction and ravishment your fertile imagination has conjured up.'

CHAPTER FOUR

BOBBIE was never afterwards entirely sure when the exact moment of capitulation came. Perhaps it had been at the first mention of his sister. Or had it come later when, suddenly too exhausted and overwrought to fight him any longer, she hadn't protested when Rod had attached a tow chain to her car and firmly set off in the direction of Greentree Farm.

And once home, she hadn't been able to raise the strength to protest when he had insisted on unloading her car while she had that hot bath and then he had made an omelette and shared it with her.

They hadn't spoken much as they had sat around the oak table in the warm cosy lounge, but she had asked Rod how he had found her.

His grey eyes had rested on her with that now familiar, amused and slightly mocking look. 'As a matter of fact I wasn't looking for you—at that stage. I'd phoned around the district earlier with no success, and when I came across you I was heading for Kilmore in a towering rage, as a matter of fact.'

'Kilmore . . .?'

'Yes, I'm putting up at the pub there.' He'd glanced at his watch and pushed back his chair. 'And right now I think I'll make tracks and let you get to bed—alone.' He'd grinned as she flushed painfully, and stood up. 'I'll be back in the morning, Bobbie. And don't devise any little plans for leaving here, because I can assure you I won't be so—contained if it happens again.' And with a careless pat for Bluey, he had left.

Or did I capitulate when he started to talk horses? she asked herself as she was again seated across the oak table from him. But now, in the light of a sunny, reasonably warm morning, you can't deny, Bobbie Hallam, that you have. And she felt an unfamiliar sinking feeling in the pit of her stomach.

'Do you mean . . . I can keep some of my horses here?' she stammered.

'Yes. That mare you drove at Kilmore was quite impressive. I had a look at them yesterday, and I also liked the chestnut colt. I reckon you're wasting your time with the others you had in work, though.'

She started to speak, but changed her mind. What could she tell him about horses? And then she flew out of the chair.

'What is it?' he demanded.

'I forgot! There's a carrier coming to pick them all up this morning. . . .'

'Don't worry about that,' he said negligently. 'I cancelled it.'

'You what?' she demanded heatedly.

'Sit down, Bobbie, and get your hackles down, for God's sake!'

She sank back into her chair. 'How did you even know. . . .'

'They rang yesterday afternoon while I was here. They wanted to let you know they couldn't manage to come today and suggested tomorrow instead. I told them not to worry.'

'Did you now?' she glared at him, but he laughed easily.

'You're awfully aggressive for such a slip of a girl, Bobbie Hallam,' he told her with an amused grin. 'You remind me of an outraged puppy. Now look,' he said, and sat forward, 'let's get down to business. Of the eight you have here, my advice to you is to keep the two I've already mentioned in work, and the old mare that's in foal. I've been looking through their papers and she's pretty well bred. And whoever chose the sire of her foal chose well. If it's a reasonable individual, you should get a decent price for it as a yearling. As for the others, I think you should advertise them for sale and in the meantime they can stay in the paddock. Right?'

Bobbie hesitated, then nodded reluctantly. It wasn't that what he said didn't make sense but his manner that annoyed her.

'Good.' He glanced at her keenly. 'Now, as to the rest of your financial business—how much do you reckon you'll have over when you've repaid the mortgage?'

She coloured. 'Not very much, I'm afraid.' And then in a small voice, 'Hardly anything at all.'

'Why is that?'

'Well, I have an outstanding bill at the feed merchant.' She swallowed and told him the figure, causing him to wince.

'Anything else?'

'Yes. Dad got the track resurfaced just before . . . he died. I still haven't paid for that completely. But that's all. I don't owe anything else.'

Rod looked up from the paper he was writing on. 'I believe you,' he said somewhat grimly. 'Tell me, when did you last have a good meal?'

Her eyes flew to his face. 'What do you mean?' she whispered.

'I mean, from what some of your friends told me and the evidence of your larder, I'm quite sure you've been living on the smell of an oil rag yourself, while your horses got the best of everything.'

Bobbie grimaced. 'I wish people would mind their own business! Anyway, it doesn't take much to feed one girl and a dog.'

He stared at her and shook his head. 'You're crazy, Bobbie. However, that's beside the point. Let's see, you won't get a great deal for those horses, but still. . . .' He did some rapid arithmetic. 'Yeah,' he said finally, 'there would be enough to trade your car and float in for a new one, or at least a sound one—car, I mean, but you'd have to part with some cash. And then there would be roughly this amount left,' he indicated a figure with his pen, 'plus what Viv and I are going to pay you in rent until the sale's finalised. You could put that into a savings account and let it earn interest for you. And in the meantime, with free board and your salary, you'd be reasonably well off. And doing the only thing you obviously know how to do.'

She nodded dumbly after a moment and felt suddenly, unbearably humiliated. There was nothing now this man did not know about her. She stared down at her rough work-hardened hands. They looked so small and forlorn lying in her lap.

An abrupt movement caused her to look up. Rod was standing over her with an unreadable expression on his face. He said tersely, 'Viv and I will move in the day after tomorrow. In the meantime, I'm having some straw delivered. Could you get eight boxes ready, please, two for you and six for myself.'

Bobbie nodded mutely and he made an impatient

sound and swung on his heel. 'I'll see you, then,' he said almost angrily, and without his usual careless pat for Bluey, walked out and a few moments later the roar of his car sounded and a swirl of gravel as it raced down the drive.

She blinked several times and wondered confusedly what had upset him so suddenly. Bluey nosed his head into lap and she sighed heavily as she fondled his silky red ears.

Vivian Simpson looked around her and laughed delightedly, then put her arms around Bobbie in a spontaneous gesture. 'What a darling little house,' she said excitedly. 'I just know I'm going to enjoy staying here. And being with you, Bobbie. You're not at all what I expected,' she added ingenuously.

'Oh?' said Bobbie with a surprised look. 'What did you expect?'

'Well, to tell you the truth, Rod was rather mysterious about you and I conjured up all sorts of weird visions!' Vivian laughed. 'But I just know we're going to get along well and I want you to know, that so far as the house goes, just tell me how you do everything, how you like everything, and we'll keep it exactly the same!'

Bobbie couldn't help smiling into the warm grey eyes, but she said with a chuckle, 'Your brother might not want. . . .'

Vivian shook her vivid brown curls. 'Bobbie, we have a clear-cut arrangement in this family. Rod may be absolute master of the horses and anything that affects them, so I can't guarantee he won't turn the stables upside down, but in the house he kowtows to me?'

Bobbie grinned. She couldn't imagine Rod Simpson

kowtowing to anyone. She said, 'Shall I show you up-stairs and you can have first pick of the bedrooms?'

Vivian enthused about her bedroom and invited Bobbie to stay and talk to her while she unpacked.

'Perhaps I should be down at the stables,' said Bobbie.

'Not today,' Vivian said firmly. 'You belong to me today. Anyway, the horses don't arrive until tomorrow and Rod said we should get acquainted before they came. Now where did I pack those hangers? Oh, here they are! Do you like this dress, Bobbie? Rod gave it to me for my birthday. I'm twenty-one whole years and two weeks.'

She pirouetted around the room with the filmy even-ing dress clutched in front of her.

'It's lovely,' Bobbie murmured.

'I thought so too. He has good taste, one can't deny it, whatever else I say about him.' Vivian stopped in front of Bobbie. 'Do you know, you have the most fabulous colouring—that hair and those eyes!'

Bobbie blushed and immediately decided you couldn't help liking Vivian Simpson, despite her brother. She said shyly, 'Red hair and freckles! I'd much rather be a statuesque brunette.'

Vivian eyed her and then burst out laughing, 'Thanks for them kind words,' she said laconically. And then, 'You really meant it too.' She shook her head. 'You know, I get quite angry with Rod. One of the things he did say about you was that you had a one-track mind. I took that to mean about him or men! Because so many girls do develop a one track-mind about him. But I sus-pect, having met you now, that it could be—say about horses, for instance?' she asked gently.

Bobbie nodded ruefully. 'Do you ... like horses, Vivian?'

'Call me Viv, Bobbie. Yes, I like horses, that's why I help Rod out, but I don't live, eat and sleep them and I try to stop Rod from doing it. It's not that easy, though,' she added with an impish laugh, 'and now with two of you in the house I can see it's going to be an uphill struggle!'

They both turned at a light tap on the door.

'Come in, Rod,' Viv called. She dropped the dress she was holding and ran to him and threw her arms around him. 'I love you, Rod,' she said mischievously, 'and I love Greentree Farm, and I'm well on the way to loving Bobbie, and I forgive you wholeheartedly for uprooting me and transplanting me as you did.'

He looked down at her lively, upturned face and said amusedly, 'I'm relieved to hear you say so, Viv. This time last week you were threatening never to talk to me again.'

'That was last week,' she said with twinkling eyes, 'but today is a different story. In fact I feel so generous towards you, I'll make you your favourite tea.'

Bobbie started and as her mind flew to the sparsely populated larder she felt her cheeks redden. With her car still out of action she had been unable to stock up on groceries. She had actually rung Mrs Mead to cadge a lift into town, but the Meads had been away. She twisted her hands in her lap and said in an agony of embarrassment, 'I'm so sorry, but I haven't been able. . . .'

Rod interrupted her, 'As a matter of fact, I had another idea. What would you two ladies say to a Chinese meal? I believe there's a restaurant in Seymour with a good reputation. What do you say, Viv? Bobbie?'

Bobbie looked down at her tweed skirt and soft green jumper and smiled ruefully to herself. This was the second time in three days she had worn this outfit. Her mother would have been very happy.

'Why the smile, Bobbie?' Rod's words broke in upon her reflections.

She looked up at him quickly and then around at the bustling restaurant. 'I was just thinking ... oh, it doesn't matter. Thank you for a lovely meal. I really enjoyed it!'

'I'm glad. Viv will enjoy going into Kilmore tomorrow and stocking up on groceries.'

She winced, and his hand covered hers as it lay on the table.

'Don't look like that, Bobbie. If it's any help I admire you for your sheer, maybe misguided, but all the same, guts.'

Vivian sat down at the table. 'What are you two discussing so earnestly?' she demanded.

'Horses,' said Rod with a wicked grin.

'Here we go again,' she sighed resignedly. 'Oh well, I suppose I should be grateful for the small respite we've had this evening.'

'Yeah,' he said lazily. 'And I reckon we should be making tracks now. It's a big day tomorrow!'

Bobbie stood back with wide eyes and bated breath as the glossy brown horse was unloaded from the truck.

This was Morningtown, a legend in his own lifetime, a horse that thousands of people flocked to see every time he set foot on a race track.

When he had his four feet firmly planted on the

ground he tossed his head and his long mane and forelock swung in the light breeze, and he surveyed the
stables and track with an almost human look of assessment in his eyes. Then he snorted and swished his tail.

Bobbie burst out laughing. 'I think he approves,' she
said delightedly.

'Looks like it,' Rod said dryly. 'You'll find he has his
ways, Bobbie. He's inquisitive to a fault and very prone
to be bossy. Don't let him put anything over you, because he'll make your life miserable if you do. Right,
can you put him in the gig for me, please? I want to jog
him a few laps to loosen him up after the trip. We'll do
them all one at a time, just a couple of laps at a slow
jog. We'll do three each. You take that lot, Bobbie.' He
gestured to three horses tied up at the hitching rail.

'Yes, boss,' she said with a happy grin, and set to
work.

It was several days later that Bobbie climbed to the top
of the hill and stood under the big tree that gave the
farm its name during her midday break. She flung herself down in the warm, softly waving grass and sighed
contentedly and plucked a long stalk of grass to chew.

I'm happy, she told herself. Really happy. Who
would have thought it possible a week ago?

'Certainly not me, Bluey,' she told the dog resting
contentedly beside her. 'If only . . . if only it could go on
like this for ever, old son, it would be perfect, wouldn't
it? But I'm not going to try and look into the future,'
she added resolutely. 'We'll just take it one day at a
time, that's what we'll do.'

She rolled on to her stomach and looked down towards the track and the stables as they lay peacefully,

bathed in the warm sunshine. Viv would be happy with the weather today, she thought idly. If there was one thing she found hard to accept about Victoria, it was the unpredictable weather. Bobbie grinned to herself and wondered what Viv's reaction would be when winter finally descended. Because to even hardened Victorians, winter came as something of a shock to the system, especially in this part of Victoria. She thought back to last winter and the number of times she had had to chip the film of ice off the horses' water first thing in the morning.

She stirred as a small red car, looking somehow toy-like from this distance, crawled off the road and down the driveway and stopped at the front door. It was the vet, she realised. Rod had had some blood samples taken and these would be the results of the tests, no doubt. She frowned for a moment. Richard Forrester, who had a flourishing equine practice in the district, didn't usually have the time to personally deliver blood tests. He normally phoned the results through—but of course! A slow grin spread across her face. Richard Forrester was tall, fair and good-looking and had a bit of a reputation as a gay bachelor, and he hadn't been unimpressed when he had been introduced to Viv. That would account for it!

Bobbie jumped up. 'Come on, Bluey,' she called. 'He'll have Bessie's test too.'

Vivian stared at the front door as it closed behind the vet, and shook her dark curls. 'I must say you Victorians are fast workers, Bobbie!'

'Who, me?' said Bobbie with raised eyebrows and an innocent little smile.

Rod raised his head from the papers he was studying.

'Correction, Bobbie,' Viv said, 'not you particularly. Your menfolk, I mean.'

'He's not my "menfolk", Viv. I doubt if he even knows I exist—I mean, not in the same way as he no doubt is aware of you,' she added demurely.

'Is that a fact?' Rod drawled. 'I thought he'd just dropped in on his way past. I can see now, though, I'll have to be getting the old shotgun out once more.'

Viv tossed her curls at him and pulled a face. 'Because you're ten years older than me, Rod Simpson, it doesn't give you the right to play heavy-handed with me! I'll pick my own boy-friends. I am twenty-one now, you know!'

He raised his eyebrows quizzically. 'I thought you were complaining about how forward he was a minute ago.'

'I was,' she said with an impudent grin, 'but I'm quite capable of putting him in his place myself. Anyway, it can't hurt to go to a dance with him. There's one coming up this Saturday at the Golf Club.' She stopped, then said excitedly, 'That's an idea! Let's all go. You haven't got anything in at Moonee Valley, have you, Rod?'

'Not this week, no. But we can't just gatecrash. . . .'

'I thought you were going to join the club?'

He laughed. 'All in good time, Viv!'

She pouted prettily, then shrugged and turned back to the stove where she was tending lunch.

Bobbie sighed with relief, but had she known Vivian better she would have realised Rod Simpson was not the only member of the family possessed of an iron determination.

She sat down at the table and he passed her a slip of paper.

'Best Dressed,' he said. 'She's a credit to you, Bobbie. Her blood's in very good order. When do you plan to start her?'

'I thought at Kilmore next week. I've nominated her already.'

'Fine,' he said. 'In the meantime I've found a car for you. It's the right price and they'll accept your car and float as a trade-in on it.'

'Oh. There's just one thing.' She looked across at him. 'How will I manage without a float?'

'I've got a float and a truck and by the time my suspension's up, which is in about ten days' time, I'll be going to most meetings, so there's no problem there.'

'Thank you,' Bobbie murmured, and he grinned at her.

'You're very meek and mild, Bobbie Hallam,' he told her.

She didn't answer. It's true, she thought to herself. It's as if all the fight's gone out of me.

But two days later, quite by accident, she discovered that this wasn't so, and she wondered afterwards how she had allowed herself to get into such a blazing row.

It had all started with Vivian's suggestion that instead of using Chris Williams for the few starters Rod had until his suspension was up, he used Bobbie.

'You're joking, Viv,' he said across the breakfast table.

'I am not,' she said flatly. 'You told me yourself she was a good little driver.'

Bobbie squirmed in her seat in an agony of embarrassment.

Viv went on. 'It would be spendid experience for her, Rod. Oh,' she shook her head in exasperation, 'I'm not suggesting you let her drive Morningtown or any of the open class horses, but these two you've got nominated at Shepperton next week—why on earth not?'

He said grimly, 'I'm pleased to hear you say that, Viv. About Morningtown, I mean. But the answer is no.'

They glared at each other. 'And why not?' demanded Vivian in an ominous tone.

'Because I don't go much on women drivers. I never have and I doubt if I ever will.'

Bobbie gasped and immediately forgot that a moment ago she had been contemplating leaving them to their argument. 'What have you got against them?' she demanded. 'I've seen women drive as well as men. It's only lack of opportunity that stops them.'

'I'm afraid I disagree with you, Bobbie,' he said coldly. 'The opportunity is there now, but how many women drivers do you see? I can only think of one top class woman you see regularly, and she's in New South Wales. We were led to believe that once the restriction on them was removed there would be a flood of them on the race track, but you could probably count them on one hand in this state.'

'It's not that long ago that the restrictions were removed,' she shot at him angrily, and Vivian gave her a surprised look as she added, 'The whole thing is, you men can't bear to think of women being able to do any-thing as well as you can!'

Rod narrowed his eyes. 'Bobbie, if you're trying to tell me you can drive as well as I can, forget it, kid.'

'Oh!' She shut her eyes in exasperation, but they flew

open at the sound of his amused chuckle. 'You're impossible!' she hissed at him. 'You know very well I wasn't trying to say that. There are not many *men* who drive as well as you do. But I can't see any earthly reason why I shouldn't one day become a competent driver.'

'Go for your life, kid. I don't question your horsemanship, but I do very much doubt your ability to stand up to the wear and tear of race driving. It's not only a question of being able to steer a horse round a track, it's so much more. You drove in one race at Kilmore that day and I saw you bring your horse back to scale. You were exhausted. I know,' he waved a hand at her, 'I know there was a lot riding on that race, but you try and do it three or four times in one meeting, let alone seven or eight times, and see how you stand up to it. It's a question of sheer physique, for one thing, not to mention the other drivers in the race that have got to be out-thought and outwitted while you've got a handful of horse to deal with. Take it from me, it's never a tea-party out there, Bobbie.' He pushed his chair back and stood up impatiently. 'Life would be a whole lot easier if women stayed at home and did the job they were put on this earth to do.'

She said through her teeth, 'I'm surprised you can bear to let me lay a hand on your horses. And will you stop calling me kid!'

'If I call you that, it's because that's how you seem to me.' His eyes were cold and angry as he turned to his sister. 'And I'll thank you not to dream up any more impossible schemes.' And he left the house without a backward glance.

Vivian waited until he was out of earshot and burst

into peals of laughter. 'Oh, Bobbie,' she gasped finally as Bobbie stared at her in bewilderment, 'I did enjoy that! Do you know, I haven't seen anyone stand up to Rod for ages. And of all people, a slip of a kid like you . . . I'm sorry,' she added hastily, 'I didn't mean the kid bit. But you were marvellous. I hope you stay with us for a long time.' She hugged Bobbie with sisterly affection. 'Cheer up, chicken! Why are you looking so glum? You've made my day.'

'And my own,' Bobbie said with a reluctant grin. 'Don't forget I've got to go down there and work with him.'

'So you have,' said Viv with another chuckle. 'But one thing about Rod, once he gets over his rage, he doesn't harbour any grudges.'

Bobbie shivered suddenly. 'That's just as well,' she said naïvely, 'because he's had the opportunity to chalk up a few to me.'

Vivian stood poised with several plates in her hands and regarded Bobbie thoughtfully for a moment. Then she turned to the sink and her voice was muffled as she said obscurely, 'Is it possible . . .?'

'Is what possible?' Bobbie asked after a moment.

'Oh, nothing,' Viv said hurriedly. She turned and gave Bobbie a bright smile. 'Better not keep him waiting!'

CHAPTER FIVE

SATURDAY dawned clear and cold. But it was the kind of day that made you feel happy to be alive, Bobbie thought as she dried down the last horse and put it in its box. The fresh, chilly air was like champagne and each blade of grass and tree in the paddocks seemed to stand out with a startling clarity.

And because she felt so happy she took Bluey for a run up the hill to the giant tree and together they savoured the splendid view before they jogged down to the house again.

Vivian looked at her flushed face and sparkling eyes as she skipped into the house and announced that she could eat a horse for lunch.

'You know, Bobbie,' she said thoughtfully, 'I do believe you've put on a bit of weight. Not too much, I hope,' she added ruefully.

Rod looked up from where he was lounging at the table, scanning the morning papers. He said negligently, 'Bobbie could put on a stone quite comfortably and I'd probably still be able to span her waist with my hands. Don't look so worried, kid, all Viv means is that you've lost that finedrawn look.'

Bobbie subsided into a chair and forebore to mention that it wasn't so much the thought of putting on weight that had worried her but the thought of his hands around her waist that had unaccountably caused her heart to bump.

Vivian put a heaped plate in front of her. 'Not horse, I'm afraid, but probably more appetising.'

'It smells delicious, Viv!' said Bobbie, and tucked in. It wasn't until she had polished off the last mouthful that she raised her head and said impishly, 'There, I bet that will add a few pounds. By the way, why did you look so worried just now?'

'Oh . . . nothing. It was nothing,' Viv said nonchalantly. 'What are you going to do now, Bobbie?'

'Well, I thought I'd be incredibly lazy and curl up on my bed with one of those books you lent me.'

'A jolly good idea,' Viv said approvingly. 'I'll even let you off the dishes today. Off you go!'

Bobbie went, but she paused with her foot on the last step of the staircase and looked down at the two of them. Vivian was smiling at her brother, who shrugged his shoulders and turned back to his newspapers.

Why do I get the feeling they're up to something? Bobbie asked herself, as she made her way down the passage to her bedroom. Oh well, she shrugged, I guess I'll find out in good time. And with a pleasant feeling of weariness she sank down on to the bed, pushed Bluey to the foot of it and opened her book.

But it wasn't long before the lines swam before her eyes and she dropped off to sleep.

It was Vivian who woke her with a gentle hand to her shoulder.

'Come on, sleepyhead! Time to have your shower and then we've got some work to do.'

Bobbie rubbed her eyes and yawned enormously, 'What do you mean, Viv?' she murmured. 'I always have my shower after we've fed the horses.'

'Well, today you're having it now. Up you get, and don't argue with me, Bobbie Hallam!'

Bobbie stood under the warm shower water with a puzzled frown on her face. She had only been half awake when Viv had pushed her into the shower, but she was now fully awake and wondering what had got into Viv.

'Something fishy going on, Bluey,' she told the patient dog as she came out of the bathroom to find him waiting for her outside the door.

She marched into her bedroom and froze. For lying spread out across her bed was an absolute dream of a dress—a full-length evening dress in a delicate straw-coloured chiffon, and next to it a petticoat, also full length, of the same colour. With dazed eyes she took in the details of the dress, long full sleeves with tight cuffs and tiny, delicate buttons that matched the buttons down the front of the finely pleated bodice, a small frilled, stand-up collar and the long sweep of the gathered skirt from a fitted waistline. And standing demurely, side by side on the floor beneath the dress, a pair of high-heeled gold sandals.

She switched her bemused gaze to Vivian, who was sitting at her dressing table with a complacent smile on her face and surrounded by a forest of creams and lotions.

'What . . . is this?' Bobbie stammered.

'The Golf Club dance,' Vivian said succinctly.

Bobbie felt a rush of pure panic. 'But I'm not going!'

'Oh yes, you are, my pet. I've spent days altering that dress for you and I specially painted and renovated an old pair of silver sandals of mine—in case you hadn't noticed, I have very small feet. As small as yours in fact. Come and sit down here.' She patted the comfortable armchair whose sole occupant was generally Raggedy-Ann. 'I'm going to do you over—a manicure, a facial and a hair-do. Believe me, it does wonders for one, Bobbie.'

'But ... but....' Bobbie spluttered, and was remorsely pushed down on top of the old doll.

'But what?'

'Look, Viv, it's awfully sweet of you, but I can't go to the dance! For one thing, I haven't got a partner and for another, I've never been to a ... do like this!'

'All the more reason to start right now. And you have got a partner. We're going as a foursome—me and Richard and you and Rod.'

'Viv!' Bobbie sprang up agitatedly. 'I'm the last person he'd want to be seen dead with at a sophisticated place like the Golf Club! I think you've gone crazy,' she added with a decided note of annoyance in her voice.

'Not half as crazy as you, Bobbie Hallam,' retorted Vivian with an exasperated shake of her curls as she pushed her back into the chair. 'For your information, going to a dance with someone doesn't mean anything these days. All it means is that he will escort you there and home and in between times you can both do as you like. Which is certainly what I shall be doing. Anyway, he didn't object when I put it to him.... What is it now?' she demanded as Bobbie sprang up again.

'You keep making me squash my doll!' Bobbie exclaimed heatedly as she rescued Raggedy-Ann and plumped her up. And then Vivian's last words sank in. 'Do you mean,' she said more slowly, 'that he knows about it?'

'Of course he knows about it. He said he thought it was a good idea, provided....'

'Provided what?'

'Provided I could persuade you!' Vivian narrowed her

eyes and glared at Bobbie. 'Do you mean to tell me I've gone to all this trouble for nothing?'

They stared at each other aggressively for a moment before Vivian said, almost cajolingly now, 'Bobbie, that dress is going to suit you so well, you won't recognise yourself. Have you ever worn a long dress like that? I tell you it's a terrific experience, your first long dress swirling around your legs. See,' she lifted the petticoat and held it in front of Bobbie, 'the petticoat has very narrow little straps so your shoulders and arms are bare under the chiffon. And the colour will make your eyes so clear and green.'

'The colour will match my freckles,' Bobbie said with a rueful grin. 'I. . . .'

'By the time I've finished with you, Bobbie, no one will notice a freckle or two. Now are you going to sit down and let me start on your nails?'

Bobbie pulled a face and sank back reluctantly. 'Viv, I really would rather. . . .'

But Vivian, sensing victory, said briskly, 'Trust me, Bobbie, will you? Now don't talk for a minute, I've got an oatmeal mask here. . . .'

Bobbie said desparingly in one last effort, 'What about the horses, though? They've still got to be fed.'

'Rod's doing it. Close your eyes and hold your head still . . . that's a good girl!'

'Oh, Viv!' was all Bobbie could say as they both stood before the long mirror in Vivian's bedroom.

It was true, Bobbie thought, as she surveyed the elegant creature in the mirror. I don't recognise myself. The beautiful dress seemed to make her look taller and invest her with subtle curves. Her hair was brushed smoothly about her face and it shone with rich auburn tints. Vivian had made her face up very delicately with a minimum of make-up, but the effect was quite startling. Her eyelashes had been darkened with mascara and looked incredibly long against her pale skin. She had just a hint of eyeshadow on and a touch of blusher and lip-gloss. Who could have thought it could make such a difference? she asked herself.

She lifted the front of the skirt and twirled slowly and was unable to suppress the eager note in her voice as she said, 'What do you think, Viv?'

'I think you look stunning, Bobbie.' She planted a quick kiss on Bobbie's cheek and gave her own dress a complacent pat. 'There,' she said as she bustled Bobbie out of the room ahead of her, 'that wasn't so bad was it?'

'No. That was fun,' Bobbie said frankly, 'but I'm not so sure about the next bit. I. . . .'

'Now come along, Roberta,' Viv said firmly but with a twinkle in her eye. 'This is no time to get cold feet. Besides, Rod will be ready and waiting and he doesn't like to be kept waiting. Here, put this wrap round your shoulders. Have you got your mother's evening purse? Good. Right, chin up, chicken, let's make a grand entrance.'

And she swept regally down the stairs with Bobbie following hesitantly behind her.

Rod was standing in the middle of the room downstairs waiting for them. Bobbie drew a quick breath and stumbled suddenly. He was immaculately dressed in a black dinner suit with a dazzling white shirt front, and his glance was curiously intent as it rested on her now flushed face as she reached the bottom of the stairs and stood for a moment.

'Well, well,' he drawled finally, and turned to his sister. 'You've created a veritable swan, Vivi. I foresee an evening spent elbowing aside a throng of admirers. And you look a treat yourself, my little sister. I chose well when I chose that dress, didn't I?'

'You did too, Rod. And see, I'm wearing your gold ear-rings as well. Shall we go? I said we'd meet Richard there at seven-thirty and it's seven o'clock now.'

Bobbie was conscious of creating a mild sensation at the Golf Club dance which gave her a warm feeling of pleasure but at the same time brought a rueful grin to her features as each old acquaintance stopped and stared, then rushed over to her in a flurry of surprise and warm greetings.

At one stage Rod said to her with a wicked glint in his eyes, 'I hope you don't intend doing a Cinderella act on me when the clock strikes midnight, Bobbie. Because all your friends are acting as if that's what they expect to happen. You know, with one wave of a magic wand you'll turn back into a. . . .'

'Into a scrubby tomboy,' she finished for him. 'They are rather surprised, aren't they?'

'And happy for you too,' he commented.

'Yes,' she said softly, and looked around her. The room was candlelit tonight and at one end a small band was playing soft music as couples danced dreamily on the small dance floor. And with a start Bobbie realised this was the first dance she had sat out all evening, and she thanked heavens for those dancing lessons her mother had insisted she take in her last year at school. She had danced with young and old alike, most of whom she had known for years. In fact there was only one person she knew in the room that she hadn't danced with, she mused. Not that he had lacked partners—as a matter of fact he had been as busy as she had. But all the same. . . .

'A penny for your thoughts, Cinderella?' His voice broke in on her reflections.

She coloured faintly and shook her head. 'Nothing really.'

'Well, in that case, and seeing that the crush of admirers has lessened, shall we dance?'

Bobbie nodded mutely and half rose, but a voice caused her sit again and she saw Rod staring at a superbly dressed blonde girl crossing the room towards them.

'Rod Simpson! Is it really you?' the girl purred and with a sensuous wiggle in her black satin dress that clung revealing to her perfect figure, she threw her arms around his neck and planted a kiss full on his lips.

'Hey, Marianne!' He untwined her arms and eased her into a chair beside him. 'What are you doing here?' he asked her laughingly as he pulled a snowy white handkerchief from his pocket and wiped his face.

'I might ask the same of you, darling. You're the last person I expected to see in this neck of the woods!'

'As a matter of fact I'm living down here now.'

'Are you ever?' Marianne asked excitedly. 'Well, what do you know—I've just moved to Melbourne myself. Isn't that something!' Her sleepy blue eyes fell on Bobbie and narrowed faintly. 'Don't tell me,' she said with one perfectly manicured finger-nail to her lips. 'I've got it! This is a niece of yours and you're chaperoning her to the dance.' She turned her blue eyes to him and smiled into his grey ones and murmured huskily, 'How perfectly sweet of you, darling.'

Rod shook his head and grinned at her wryly. 'I don't think I'm quite old enough to be Bobbie's uncle. Marianne, this is Bobbie Hallam, she's ... well, you could say she's a partner of mine. Bobbie, this is Marianne Hunter.'

'How do you do,' Bobbie murmured, and shivered inwardly as Marianne shot her a cold piercing look from under her lashes. She wondered what she'd done to deserve such a look.

Just at that moment a young man she had known since kindergarten approached and asked her to dance, and she stood up with a feeling of relief. 'Would you excuse me?' she asked.

'Sure, Bobbie, go ahead,' said Rod, and turned back to the sultry blonde, and the last words Bobbie heard as she followed her partner on to the floor were Marianne's.

'Darling, it's just going to be like old times, isn't it?'

Michael Findlay seemed to be having some difficulty keeping his feet, Bobbie, noted as he tripped over hers for the sixth time.

She said with a laugh, 'Oh, Mike! I think you've had too much to drink!'

He grinned at her a trifle hazily. 'I can't believe it's really you, Bobbie Hallam. Do you remember the day you fell in the creek and I fish ... fished you out?'

'I do so, Mike,' she said with another laugh. 'And I also remember it was you who pushed me in.'

He stumbled against her and stood on her toe once more.

'Mike,' she said more soberly, 'I think you ought to sit down.'

'What ... what I need is a breath of fresh air. Come

out on the verandah with me, Bobbie?'

'Well——' she hesitated. 'Oh, all right. But I'm not staying out there,' she told him firmly. 'It'll be freezing.'

Somehow they negotiated the tables and stepped out through the french doors.

Mike took a deep gulp of the fresh, cold air and turned to her. 'That's better,' he said, but she noticed that he was still not very sure on his feet.

He said, 'You could have knocked me down with a feather, Bobbie, when I saw you tonight. Who would have thought such a skinny little thing could turn out like this? You know, I always thought you lived for horses, but I wonder now.'

'Wonder what?' she asked tartly.

'Wonder . . . who all this finery is for.' He fingered the sleeve of her dress. 'C-could it be that the great Rod Simpson has made another c-conquest?'

Bobbie stared at him and said bitterly, 'You haven't changed, have you, Mike? You were thoroughly nasty when you pushed me into the creek, and you're still the same.'

He swayed on his feet but said quite clearly, 'And you were always a little wildcat dead set on bossing everyone around. But tonight we'll see who's boss!'

And with a lurch he grabbed her, and she shrivelled with revulsion as his hot, beer-laden breath fanned her cheeks and his hungry mouth sought her own.

'Mike . . .!' But she got no farther as his lips pressed on hers, and suddenly she came alive in his arms and fought with all her strength and using her teeth and nails.

He lifted his head briefly and murmured, 'Cut it out, Bobbie.'

'I will not . . .!' she panted, and drove the slender heel of her sandal into his shoe.

Mike staggered and clutched at her. 'You little bitch!' he muttered through clenched teeth. 'You'll pay for that!' And above the heaving of her own breath she heard an ominous ripping sound and realised his clutching hands had torn her dress.

'Let me *go!*' She got her hands up to his face, but he only laughed at her and once again his lips found hers.

And then all of a sudden he was no longer holding her but lying flat on his back on the wooden verandah floor, and Bobbie was staring into Rod Simpson's cold grey eyes as she desperately tried to cover her exposed shoulder where her dress had ripped.

'Don't you know anything, Bobbie Hallam?' Rod demanded angrily.

She jumped at the harsh words and inexplicably her tongue seemed to tie itself in knots. 'I . . . he . . . we. . . .'

He made an impatient sound and said roughly, 'Go round the verandah to the car park. Here.' He handed her his car keys. 'I'll meet you there in a minute. You can't go back inside like that.' He turned decisively and went in through the french doors.

Bobbie cast the groaning figure still lying supine on the floor an agonised glance and then with one hand to her skirt and the other to the torn shoulder of her dress, she fled along the verandah towards the car park.

Rod was as good as his word, and she had barely settled herself in the front seat than he appeared and got in himself, tossing her stole and bag into her lap. She picked the stole up with trembling fingers and arranged it round her shoulders. The powerful engine under the long sleek bonnet roared to life and with a swish of gravel they turned out of the car park and on to the road.

Bobbie peeped at Rod once from under her lashes as he drove the car through the night at a frightening speed. Why was he so angry with her? she asked herself. Because one glance at the stern set of his features confirmed that he was still furiously angry.

She plucked at the delicate material of her skirt with agitated fingers, wanting desperately to speak, but the words wouldn't come and they drove the whole way home in a frigid silence.

Surely he doesn't think I was encouraging Mike? Surely he couldn't be thinking that? She shivered suddenly as he brought the car to a juddering halt outside the front door.

'Out,' said Rod briefly. 'I'm just going to put the car away.'

She stumbled out and stood shivering on the doorstep while he parked the car because he had the key.

He made another impatient sound when he found her still standing on the doorstep.

'Here,' he said as he unlocked the door, 'in you go.'

Bobbie straightened her shoulders and marched in ahead of him with her head held high. She turned to face him with as much hauteur as she could muster as he slammed the door behind him.

'I don't know what you're so upset about——' she began furiously.

'Well, I'll tell you,' he said softly, menacingly, and advanced towards her. 'You must have realised he was drunk not very long after you first started to dance with him. It was certainly obvious to me when I turned round to watch you. If I hadn't been . . . otherwise en-

gaged I'd have come over there and then. Can you imagine my acute surprise when not two minutes later,
however, you'd both disappeared? I couldn't believe
you would be so stupid to allow yourself to be tricked
out on to the verandah by a drunken lout! You were
only asking for trouble—which you got in good measure, I see.' His eyes rested on her bruised lips and then
travelled slowly down to her shoulder and the torn
dress. 'It's about time you grew up, Bobbie Hallam.'

'You've got it all wrong,' she said hotly. 'I've known
Mike Findlay for as long as I can remember! We went
to school together, we've driven against each other at
shows and trials and he's never once . . . led me to think
. . . he'd behave like that! The only reason I went outside with him was because—well, because, as I said, I've
known him a long time and I was afraid he was going
to pass out on the dance floor and make a fool of himself. He was never one of my favourite people,' she said
candidly, 'but all the same. . . . And I had no idea he
was going to leap on me like that!' She stuck her chin
out aggressively. 'In any case, who are you to pass judg-
ment on me like some . . . some higher being?'

But although the words were brave she couldn't prevent a tiny gasp of fright as Rod towered over her with
such a look of blazing fury in his eyes. She stood her
ground, though, and glared up at him, although under-
neath the bravado she was actually trembling with
fright.

'You little fool,' he muttered somewhat indistinctly,
and took her shoulders in a bruising grasp. 'For the
first time in your life you appear dressed as a girl and
yet you expect everyone still to treat you like some . . .
stablehand they're so used to seeing around they never

think twice about! It's about time you stopped thinking like a silly schoolgirl, because if you don't you'll find yourself constantly in trouble, and I might not always be around to rescue you. Or perhaps you enjoy having drunken louts trying to make love to you?'

'Oh! How dare you!' she spat at him, and tried to wrench her arms free, but he merely tightened his grip and she heard again that ominous ripping sound.

'Now look what you've done!' she stormed at him with angry tears in her eyes. '*You've* gone and made me tear my dress! And it was such a lovely dress. I hate you!' she added with a sob in her voice. 'I hate all of you . . . men!'

His grip slackened immediately and the look of anger left his eyes, to be replaced by an unfathomable expression. He let his hands slide down her arms, but gently now, and he took both her hands in his.

'Look at me, Bobbie,' he said.

'I am,' she replied bitterly. 'Will you please let me go?'

'Very well.' He released her hands and she turned immediately and with a forlorn attempt at dignity pulled the stole around her and started towards the staircase.

'Bobbie.'

She stopped with her foot on the bottom step but obstinately refused to turn towards him.

'Bobbie,' he said again.

'What is it now?' she whispered.

'I'm sorry. I said some unforgivable things.'

'That's all right,' she said gruffly after a moment, and passed a wrist over her brimming eyes. 'If you don't mind I think I'll go to bed now. Oh!' She turned to him. 'What about Viv? I forgot about her.'

'Her cavalier, the vet, is bringing her home.'

'Oh,' she said again. 'Well, goodnight.'

But with one swift movement Rod was beside her. 'Just a minute,' he said with a suspicion of a laugh in his voice.

She looked up at him. 'What ... what is it?'

'It's this.' He took her in his arms before she realised what he was about. She took a faltering breath and stared up at him, unable to move and unable to still the sudden hammering of her heart.

He said softly, 'No young girl's first dance should end like this.' He brought one hand up and tipped her head back with a gentle pressure under her chin. 'Will you accept this as a tribute to an exceptionally lovely young girl from a rather ... seasoned bachelor? You were a sight to gladden most men's eyes tonight.' And with the gentlest pressure, his lips rested briefly on her own. 'There.' He lifted his head and said with a teasing grin. 'Was that so hateful?'

Bobbie shook her head mutely, and he released her and said,

'I think it's time for bed, Cinderella!'

CHAPTER SIX

BOBBIE worked through the next morning as if in a trance. For the night had brought strange, troubling revelations to her and made her realise just how fragile her happiness and peace of mind had been.

Oh, I *am* just a silly schoolgirl, she told herself for the tenth time as she mixed the midday feeds. It's simply an adolescent crush you've got on him and the sooner you get over it the better, Bobbie Hallam! Because despite or even because of his gentle kiss last night, you must realise that it was only the action of a sophisticated man to make you feel better. You'll probably always be just a scrubby tomboy to him. And her thoughts strayed to the gorgeous, equally sophisticated Marianne Hunter. She's definitely more in his line she told herself and sighed suddenly. And realised she'd mixed two extra feeds while she'd been day-dreaming.

Now you've got to stop this, she told herself sternly as she carried the feed buckets to the impatient horses. Because if you don't, he'll realise what's up, and that would be awful. Then I'd have to go.

Morningtown whinnied at her as she passed his door.

'Hang on a sec! I'm coming with yours now,' she told him. 'And don't eat it so fast, will you, because you'll give yourself colic one day.' And she had to laugh as she poured his feed into his bin over his impatient nose. She put the bucket down and played with his forelock as he chomped greedily. 'You're just like a big kid, you know,' she said softly. 'Just you wait until you have your first start down here. You're going to shine after I've finished grooming you, like you've never shone before. Just like the champion you are.'

Vivian was obviously curious about Bobbie's abrupt departure from the dance, and as they sat down to lunch on their own she demanded to be told all about it.

'Rod just ignored me when I asked him,' she said plaintively, 'and you must have gone down to the stables at the crack of dawn! I'd just like to know what's going on!'

'Where is Rod?' Bobbie asked.

'He got a mysterious phone call this morning. He's gone out to lunch.'

Bobbie relaxed slightly and told Vivian what had taken place last night.

'Oh, Bobbie, how awful for you! I'm so sorry.' She paused. 'But why was Rod so angry?'

'He thought I should have known better.'

Vivian grimaced. 'Anyone with a pair of eyes in their head would have realised you wouldn't have encouraged him. Really, I don't understand men sometimes—even Rod. I've got a very strong suspicion his mystery caller this morning was that Hunter female. Now in most respects Rod is a reasonably rational male, yet how come he can be taken in by a . . . a shameless hussy like that? I ask you!'

Bobbie laughed. 'It's no good asking me, Viv. Don't you . . . like her?'

'I do not!' Vivian said roundly. 'She reminds me of a man-eating shark. And what's more, I don't for one minute believe that she didn't know Rod had moved

down here. I think she's pursued him. She was one of
the reasons I *was* glad to leave New South Wales. She
hasn't given him a minute's peace since she first laid
eyes on him. Can you imagine having a sister-in-law
like that? It's enough to give you the cold shivers!' she
said dramatically.

. 'Is he ... do you think he's serious about her?'
Bobbie asked reluctantly.

Vivian pulled a face. 'I'm hoping not. He generally
has no difficulty in loving 'em and leaving 'em,' she
added with a tinge of irony. 'But Marianne's particularly persistent.' She added with a sigh, 'And you've
got to admit she's quite gorgeous—on the outside, that
is.'

Bobbie spent the afternoon polishing Best Dressed's
harness for the races tomorrow and then she pressed
her white trousers and colours.

Rod still hadn't returned by tea-time, so she and
Vivian fed the horses and did all the evening chores and
finally sat down to tea on their own.

Bobbie said as they dried the dishes, 'I forgot to ask
you how you enjoyed the dance, Viv.'

Vivian was silent for a moment, then she said with a
curiously wry note in her voice, 'Have you ever been
swept off your feet, Bobbie? I mean, met a man one day
and fallen in love with him the next? No, I don't suppose you have, love—yet. But I'm horribly afraid that's
what's happened to me.'

Bobbie stopped drying and stared at her. 'Do you
mean Richard?'

'Yes. And I'm afraid it's come as rather a blow to my
ego. You see, I've always had a mental picture of myself

as being very cool and logical—you know, perfectly in command of my own life. But I've got this awful feeling that if he were to ask me to marry him tomorrow I'd do it without a second thought.'

'Viv! You've only. . . .'

'I know, I know, I've only just met him. But to me he's like all my dreams rolled into one.'

'But how can you know?'

'That's what I keep asking myself.' Vivian sat down at the table with a dreamy expression on her face. 'He's—how can I explain it? He's sort of sure of himself and he doesn't have to put on a false air of bravado like so many men do, if you know what I mean. He's . . . well, he's like Rod in that respect. You get the feeling he's grown up, and in the nicest possible way.' She grinned up at Bobbie's startled face. 'The million-dollar question, though, is, does he feel the same way about me?'

Bobbie sat down too.

'Don't look so worried, Bobbie,' said Viv with a chuckle.

'Well—I mean, he's—Richard, I mean. . . .'

'Are you trying to tell me he's something of a gay bachelor?'

'Well, so far as I know, in a nice way—yes.' Bobbie sought for the right words. 'What I mean is, I've never heard any horrible stories about him at all, but— well. . . .' She paused and then said with a rush, 'You so often see him with a different girl-friend.'

'I suppose you could say the same about Rod, and for that matter I've had a few beaux myself. But you see I just know, with Rod anyway, when the right one comes along for him, he'll be a dedicated husband because he never does *anything* in half measures. And the girl he does finally choose will be a very lucky girl—that's why I'm so anxious for him to choose the right one. But if his wife didn't ... share that same dedication,' Vivian paused and shivered slightly, 'I think he could be very cruel. And that's how I see Richard too. And if the way I feel about him is any guide at all, I reckon I could make a very dedicated wife.' She stared almost sombrely across the room. 'All I know is, Bobbie, I've never felt this way before in my life. It must mean something.'

Bobbie pondered this as she prepared for bed that night, and had to admit ruefully that she understood exactly how Vivian felt. Because she herself felt the same way about Rod.

'Only difference, Bluey old son, is I do suspect Richard Forrester might be just as stuck on Vivian as she is on him.'

Her thoughts roamed back to the dance as she sat at the dressing table and brushed her hair. He had certainly been watching Vivian whenever she had danced with somebody else.

The sound of a car in the driveway caused her to jump. That must be Rod coming home at last. She sprang up and switched off the light and jumped into bed. Bluey thumped his tail on the quilt and whined softly.

'I'm not letting you out, old son,' she told him sternly, 'although I suspect you're every bit as keen on the boss as. . . .' She stopped and shook herself impatiently. Enough of that, she told herself equally sternly, and pulled the covers over her ears. Think about tomorrow and the race.

But all the same she heard each footprint downstairs and then finally on the stairs and down the passageway.

Monday was cold and wet. Vivian shook her head impatiently as she surveyed the dismal drizzle outside.

'Will they still race, Bobbie?' she asked.

'Of course.' Bobbie looked surprised. 'It takes a great deal more than this to put the races off.'

Vivian pulled a face. 'Rather you than me, Bobbie. You'll be covered in grit by the time you get off the track.'

Rod looked up. 'They're a hardy bunch down this part of the world, Viv. And if they allowed themselves to be put off by a little drizzle, they'd never get anything done. Isn't that so, Bobbie?'

'I guess so,' Bobbie said with a laugh. 'You get so used to it, you see. And when a fine day comes along you really appreciate it.'

But despite her words, Bobbie felt a twinge of annoyance herself at the weather as she headed Bess out on to the track. The rain was now falling quite heavily, although still not heavily enough to allow the race to be abandoned. Just enough to make it unpleasant and awkward. In fact, all in all, Bobbie was feeling unusually tense.

It had all started with Rod's insistence that Bluey be left at home. She hadn't liked to argue with him because they were using his car, but the sight of Bluey's mournful face at the window as they drove off had upset her. But even this was a minor irritation compared to what awaited her at the track—Marianne Hunter, looking superbly elegant in beautifully cut slacks, a bright rain jacket and a jaunty cap. One look at Vivian's face had been enough to confirm that Bobbie wasn't the only female to be immediately made conscious of a feeling of dowdiness.

However, this was a fleeting sensation, Bobbie discovered when confronted by Marianne's reaction to the news that Bobbie was actually driving in a race.

'How ... perfectly quaint!' she had drawled as if Bobbie was some sort of sub-species.

Bobbie had gritted her teeth and muttered to Vivian, 'Please ... just keep her away from me.'

'Right!' Vivian had replied, and with as much tact as a sergeant-major she had firmly shepherded Marianne away.

But Rod had stayed to say grimly, 'This damn rain! Have you ever driven in the rain before?'

'Plenty of times,' Bobbie had replied shortly and with a certain disregard for the truth. She had driven fast work innumerable times at home in heavier rain than this, but never in a race with eleven other horses. However, she saw no reason to enlighten him about this.

'Well, take care,' he had said. 'And forget about winning this race, because the most important thing is to get the horse around safely.'

As if I wouldn't, she told herself angrily. I mean, take care of the horse. What does he think I am? And she jogged Bess down the back straight towards the start and wiggled in the seat as the rain dripped off the back of her helmet and with a devastating cunning found the gap between her waterproof colours and her neck.

The starter called the field up and Bobbie lined up on the second line next to Ted Wilson, who gave her a cheery wave. She turned to the other side and was conscious of a start of surprise, because seated in the gig next to her was Michael Findlay. Her mind flashed back to the list of horses and drivers. She was positive he hadn't been on it. He must be a late change, she thought with another surge of irritation as he cast her an unpleasant grin.

The starter raised his arm and with a swoosh the tapes flew back and the field was released. And Bobbie forgot about Findlay and everything else as she jockeyed for a position and landed one out and three back.

She was congratulating herself on this as the field swept out of front straight. If she could maintain this position until the last four hundred metres she had a fair chance of winning the race.

Provided, that is, she told herself breathlessly, I can see where I'm going—and gasped as the field flew through a particularly wet patch down the back straight and she found herself blinded by a shower of wet particles despite her wire mesh goggles. She raised a hand to wipe them, but the damp sand was coming up in a steady stream now from beneath those pounding hooves and gig wheels in front of her, and with an impatient gesture she slipped them down and narrowed her eyes against the flying grit.

The rain seemed to be hammering down now and she hunched up in the gig seat, concentrating desperately on one thing alone—being able to see where she was going.

It was as they swept down the back straight for the last time that she felt the bump. She looked across to her inside and through the driving rain she could dimly discern the driver. It was Michael Findlay.

'Hey!' she yelled out to him. 'What do you think you're doing?'

If he replied, she didn't hear it, but she saw his horse

edge out again towards Bess and felt his gig wheel contact her own. And she suddenly realised how true the old saying about seeing red was. All the accumulated irritations of the morning rose up within her as she shortened her grip on the left rein and hauled Best Dressed's head to one side until the two horses were racing shoulder to shoulder.

She heard Michael's hoarse shout as his horse stumbled and then went up in the air and came down galloping in its hopples. She immediately drew on the other rein and pulled Bess out and scooted round the field as it swept into the front straight. And she was conscious of a thrill as she realised she had caught everyone napping and Bess surged effortlessly to the lead through the driving rain and passed the post with a couple of lengths to spare.

It was then that Bobbie came to grief. As she pulled the mare up, Bess skidded suddenly and with a surprised cry Bobbie found the gig tilting sideways beneath her, then she was sitting on the track amidst a welter of horses and gigs as the field behind her, with a great deal of shouting and manipulation, made a concerted and strenuous effort to avoid her.

She held her breath and shrank into herself, unable to move a muscle until the last horse had passed. Then she got to her knees and looked around in trepidation—and breathed a deep sigh of relief. No one else, so far as she could see in the murky light, had fallen, and even Bess was still upright and in the capable hands of the clerk of the course.

Bobbie let out a trembling sigh. But whenever she thought of the whole business afterwards, she was never quite sure what had embarrassed her most, the actual fall or the incident afterwards. For just as she was climbing to her feet, a figure loomed out of the rain and grabbed her by the shoulders and hauled her upright. Somehow she knew it was Rod before she glimpsed his angry grey eyes.

'What the hell did you think you were doing?' he demanded furiously, and shook her. 'You came down the straight like a bat out of hell, yet I doubt if you could see a foot in front of you. Are you quite crazy?'

'I . . . but I won,' she said stupidly.

'Yes, you won, and nearly killed yourself in the process, you little idiot! The track's like a skateway now—didn't you realise that?' He shook her again and she felt her teeth rattle together. 'And just what were you doing in the back straight? You all but tipped Findlay out.'

'Because he was trying to tip me out!' she snapped through clenched teeth. 'Will you . . . will you let go of me! Everybody's staring. . . .'

'Let them stare,' he said contemptuously. 'You don't deserve to have a licence. It's a miracle you didn't bring the whole field down. . . .'

But his next words went right over her head, because she found to her dismay that a wave of dizziness had attacked her and she staggered suddenly beneath his hands and would have fallen had he not subjected her to the final indignity. With an impatient exclamation he scooped her up into his arms as if she weighed nothing at all, and the last thing she was conscious of was Michael Findlay's leering face and insulting whistle as he drove his horse past them.

The rest of the meeting passed in a curious blur for Bobbie. As soon as she recovered from her faint and it was decided she had sustained no injury, she was re-

quired to front the stewards and explain just what she
had been doing in the back straight, because Michael
Findlay had levelled a charge of dangerous driving
against her.

Luckily between the first-aid room and the stewards
room she caught a glimpse of Marianne Hunter, who
was regarding her with a supercilious smile on her face,
and Bobbie found this did a good deal to restore her
fighting spirits and consequently she marched into the
stewards and laid exactly the same charges against
Mike.

And possibly luckily for them both, on account of the
driving rain which had diminished the stewards' vision
of the incident, they both escaped with a severe caution,
and Bobbie received an added warning to exercise
proper care and attention at all times when on the
track, even after the winning post.

They came out of the room together but in a furious
silence, until Mike said, 'What's it to be now, Carrots?
Home to bed with the boy-friend?'

Bobbie turned on him, 'You have a filthy mind and a
filthy mouth, Mike! I'm only sorry I didn't put you over
the fence while I was about it.' She drew back her arm
to deliver a stinging blow to his cheek, but her arm was
caught in a strong grasp and she swung round to find
Rod beside her, his eyes still cold and angry.

Mike laughed unpleasantly and turned away.

'Bobbie,' Rod said between his teeth, 'haven't you
done enough damage for one day? You could get yourself suspended or disqualified if you get into a fight. Is
that something else you didn't know?'

'I don't have to take his . . . insults,' she said hotly,
'wherever I am!'

'What did he say?'

'. . . Nothing,' she said gruffly. She looked down at herself and then ruefully up at the now clearing sky.

'Yes,' he said as if reading her mind. He looked her up and down. 'You're in a right state, aren't you? You'll need a paint scraper to get the mud off you. I was going to suggest a meal, but on second thoughts a bath might be more appropriate. We'd better head for home.'

'Oh, Rod!' They both turned at the sound of Marianne's voice. She slid her arm through Rod's. 'You're not going home now, are you? The weather's clearing and there are still four more races to go.'

He hesitated briefly. 'I'm afraid so, Marianne. Bobbie's got a few grazes and scratches as well as this liberal coating of mud. She can't be feeling very comfortable.'

'But what about me, darling?' Marianne pouted. 'Are you just going to abandon me here?'

'Tell you what,' he said, 'why don't you follow us home in your car?'

Marianne's pout changed to a look of sparkling eagerness. 'I'd love that,' she gushed, and Bobbie shuddered inwardly.

'Don't worry,' she said hastily. 'I'll load Best Dressed for you and I see Mrs Mead over there, she'll be going home now because her kids are due home from school soon. She'll give me a lift. You two stay and enjoy the rest of the day.'

And with a quick wave she left them hurriedly.

Mrs Mead was a motherly, practical soul and she gave Bobbie a hand to load Best Dressed into the float and stow all the gear.

'There.' Bobbie stood back. 'All he has to do now is drive her home. I didn't want to interupt his day,' she explained.

'What's he like, Bobbie? I mean, to live with?' Mrs Mead asked as they climbed into her car. 'He was certainly concerned when you bit the dust—the mud, rather. He was over the fence before you could say Jack Robinson. Would you look at that sunshine? Why couldn't it have been shining when your race was on?'

Bobbie sat back as they passed through the little township of Kilmore while Mrs Mead rambled on from one topic to another, knowing that she very rarely required an answer to any of her questions.

A long soak in the tub achieved a remarkable transformation for Bobbie both in spirits and in appearance, and she donned the inevitable jeans and jumper and made her way down to the stables to start on the evening chores.

She was so engrossed in giving Morningtown his nightly brush and hoof treatment that she didn't hear the car and float draw up outside, and when Rod appeared with Best Dressed she started and dropped her brush.

He cast her an ironic glance as he passed down the passageway with the mare and Morningtown chose that moment to stir restlessly and upset the bucket of hoof-dressing.

'Now look what you've done!' Bobbie scolded him gently. 'Anyone would think you'd never seen her before!'

She turned to find Rod standing behind her. 'I'll do the rest, Bobbie,' he said quietly.

'Oh, look, I don't mind,' she protested.

'Well, I do. You've done more than enough for one day. And Viv's gone out to tea, so I've bought us a pizza. Perhaps you could go up and make a salad to go with it.'

She glanced at him fleetingly, not sure quite what his mood was, and said, 'I can still do that after I've helped you down here.'

'Bobbie, don't argue with me, will you?' He raised a hand. 'Any girl who's been tipped out, not to mention engaging in a bumping duel and a verbal duel—plus taking on the stewards and to cap it all being rather rude to Marianne—I'm afraid my patience is wearing very thin.'

'I wasn't being rude to her!' protested Bobbie with an innocent look.

'Oh yes, you were. Do you know what you need, Bobbie Hallam? You need a husband and some babies to look after. Otherwise you're going to grow up into a virago. . . .'

But she didn't hear any more because as her colour mounted she fled up towards the house.

CHAPTER SEVEN

THE next few weeks passed uneventfully, for Bobbie at least. She had no further confrontations with Rod, although she was painfully aware of him all the time. But they were extremely busy weeks, with Rod back driving now that his suspension was up and so many race meetings to attend. He had enlarged his team to ten horses, which meant that with her own two, they had a full stable. Twelve horses in full work took up a great deal of time, for which Bobbie was grateful, but even so there were times, usually at night when she was in bed with only Bluey for company, when she couldn't control her thoughts and dreams.

She tried to tell herself resolutely that it was the close proximity that caused her to be still as star-struck as ever. How could she get over this adolescent crush when everywhere she turned Rod was there? And doing the things that in her own small closed world represented the highest pinnacle of achievement. As if it wasn't bad enough to have him living in her house, it was a special source of penance to see his strong, lithe body in a gig behind a horse, driving with a sureness of touch that she knew in her innermost heart she could never achieve. To see him come back from working a particularly headstrong horse with a grin on his face was a source of equal pain and pleasure to her.

'In fact,' she told Bluey one night, 'I'm in a horrible position, old son. Because you see I can't work out whether it's better to at least be here, however hopeless it is, or to be away . . . and never see him again.'

Bluey thumped his tail and slid his head into her lap.

She went on as she fondled his ears, 'When I see him with Marianne, I just want to go away for ever and hide. But on the other hand, when it's just the two of us, working together, I . . . well, I'm so happy, Bluey, I'd just like it to go on for ever.' She grimaced. 'What an idiot I am!'

Bluey whined softly and Bobbie went on, 'I know exactly how you feel about him, you don't need to tell me.' She added reproachfully, 'You didn't even put up a fight!'

But if Bobbie was caught on the horns of a dilemma, it was obvious that Vivian was not. Always an attractive, vivacious girl, she now glowed with a special radiance, and Richard Forrester's little red car seemed to have become a semi-permanent fixture outside the front door of Greentree Farm.

Bobbie, who had known him for several years but never well, found that she liked him very much, and it was obvious that despite his previous track record, he was very much in love with Vivian.

She wondered idly on a couple of occasions how Rod would feel if Vivian decided to marry Richard, and concluded that as he seemed to get along with him really well, he wouldn't object.

And when the blow fell, she couldn't understand why she hadn't anticipated it in her idle musings.

The day began well enough with a work session before breakfast as usual, but from then on everything started to go wrong.

Geoffrey Goddard, the solicitor, arrived just after they finished breakfast, and with a jolt Bobbie realised that the sale of the farm must now be finalised.

It was not, as she told herself, that it was anything unexpected, but all the same it conjured up the images of her dead parents, and it was with a rather set, white face that she witnessed the handing of all the relevant papers to Rod and Vivian and accepted from the solicitor on their behalf a cheque for a sizeable amount.

Rod glanced at her keenly as he said, 'Bobbie, Viv and I can handle things today. I imagine you'd like some time off to sort out your affairs.'

'Thanks. If you don't mind, I ought to go to town.'

'While you're there, Bobbie, why don't you go into the garage and have a look at the car I was telling you about? If you like it you might as well buy it and trade your car in at the same time. The sooner you get rid of it the better. I don't place much dependance on the temporary repairs I effected.'

Bobbie nodded mutely, for the thought of parting with the old car brought to mind another set of memories—the day her father had bought it and the whole family's combined pleasure in it. Consequently she was feeling rather low as she set out for Kilmore, and this was heightened by Bluey's behaviour. He elected to stay behind with Rod.

But she had to admit, as she drove home in the little yellow car Rod had picked out for her, to a feeling of relief. The cheque from Moreton Holdings had been a bank cheque, so she had been able to draw against it immediately and settle her outstanding bill at the feed merchant and fully pay off the repairs to the track, and of course settle the mortgage on the farm. She had also negotiated to trade in her float as well as the old car for the new one and had opened a savings account for the balance of her money.

There's no doubt about it, she told herself as she steered the unfamiliar little car along the country roads, being solvent again does give one a good feeling. And of course there was the added bonus of Best Dressed's winning prize money—if only it had come a little earlier. Now, Bobbie, she told herself sternly, you know it would only have prolonged the agony. Stop being silly!

But she couldn't prevent a small curious feeling of desolation as she turned into Greentree Farm. I let it go, she thought ruefully. I just wasn't up to the challenge. Oh well. . . .

Bluey took exception to the strange car, and then when he realised who was in it, it was as if he was conscious of a double betrayal, for he made a tremendous fuss of her.

'Down, Bluey,' she gasped finally with a laugh. 'Anyone would think I'd been away for a year!'

She was still laughing as she got inside the front door with the excited dog on her heels, only to be pounced on by Vivian.

'Bobbie! Oh, Bobbie, look at this, will you!' And she thrust her left hand into Bobbie's face. 'Isn't it gorgeous? Don't you just love it?'

'It' was a diamond engagement ring.

'Viv! Congratulations!' Bobbie hugged her warmly. 'Yes, I think it's perfect. But when did this happen?'

'This afternoon, Bobbie, while you were in town. Oh, I'm so excited I could die! Richard's just left.'

Rod looked up from the table and winked at Bobbie. He said wryly, 'I wouldn't die just yet, Vivi, if I were you. Your fiancé might not appreciate it.'

'Rod,' she turned to him, 'there's something I haven't told you yet. Just a sec, I'll make Bobbie a cup of tea, she must be parched. Sit down, Bobbie, this calls for a discussion.'

Rod grimaced. 'Sounds ominous,' he said. 'Don't tell me Richard's gone bush and is demanding a bridal dowry?'

Vivian shook her brown curls at him as she poured the tea. 'It wasn't so long ago that you told me you'd be happy to pay someone to take me off your hands, Rod Simpson!'

He raised his brows. 'Did I say that? It must have been during one of our little . . . disagreements.'

'As a matter of fact, it wasn't so little,' Vivian said impishly. 'But I don't hold grudges,' she added magnanimously. 'No, it's nothing like that.' She sat down and looked at them both in turn as if she didn't quite know how to begin. Finally she said in a wheedling voice, 'Rod, you remember Aunt Victoria?'

He snorted. 'I'll never forget her, the interfering old . . . well, never mind.' He glanced at Bobbie. 'She's our father's cousin, Bobbie. She descended on us for three months a couple of years back and nearly drove me out of my mind—a dedicated spinster with a positive penchant for creating trouble. We never did see eye to eye and I doubt if we ever will. Don't tell me she wants to come and stay, Viv? Because if she does you can write and tell her the absolute truth: we don't have room for her.'

Vivian looked crestfallen. She said slowly. 'But you see, Rod, that's just it. After next week you will have room.'

Her words fell into a sudden pool of silence.

Rod narrowed his eyes and said after a moment, 'Just what do you mean by next week, Viv?'

'Well, it's like this,' said Vivian a shade unhappily.

'Richard's been offered a post at the University of Western Australia. He's ... already sold his practice here and ... and we planned to get married on Saturday, have a week's honeymoon and then,' she faltered, 'and then fly to Perth to take up this post.'

Rod stood up abruptly and swore fluently. 'It's all a bit sudden, isn't it?' he said finally with a cold look in his eye.

'Not really, Rod,' Vivian protested. 'I've known him for nearly two months now.'

'Two whole months,' Rod commented dryly. 'That's not a very long time, Viv.'

'Rod,' she said quietly with sudden tears sparkling on her lashes, 'it's long enough for me. Are you saying now you don't approve of me marrying Richard?'

Bobbie held her breath as Rod paced up and down.

He said quietly but with a steely note in his voice, 'I don't have the right to hold you back, Viv. But as a very ... loving brother, I'd hate to see you make a mistake of this magnitude because you're being rushed into it. I anticipated an engagement of, say,' he shrugged, 'three months perhaps. It could do no harm.' He stopped pacing and stared at her.

Vivian said quietly, 'That's what Richard suggested himself. But I'm just not the type to sit around and twiddle my thumbs for three months.'

She lifted her chin and returned his stare, and Bobbie was more than ever conscious of how alike these two were, not only physically but in their determination.

Vivian went on in a small but firm voice, 'I appreciate your concern, Rod, and you will always be my ... much loved and respected brother. But I know I'm right in this, and I shall do it.'

He held her gaze for a long moment and then said

with a suspicion of a sigh, 'Very well, Viv.' He sat down again and Bobbie's heart suddenly ached for both of them. She watched him anxiously, but his eyelids were lowered and his face unreadable and then suddenly his lashes lifted and he said with a wry grin, 'Well, what are we waiting for? Get out the glasses, Viv, and we shall have a drink to toast the bride-to-be!'

'Oh, Rod!' Vivian rushed round to him and threw her arms about him as the tears poured down her cheeks.

'What's this?' he said as he pinched her cheek gently. 'Happy tears, I hope?'

'Yes—well, both, I guess,' said Vivian with a sniff. 'I shall miss you so much. And you, Bobbie.' She blew her nose and then said with her old impishness, 'About Aunt Victoria . . .?'

'Forget her,' said Rod immediately, with just a touch of irritation. 'I'll . . . think of something.'

The next few days flew by in a whirl of activity. Vivian had decided to have the wedding at the farm and she had engaged a firm of caterers for the reception afterwards. Much of her time was spent in Melbourne getting her trousseau together, and one day she dragged Bobbie in with her to choose a dress to wear. She had insisted on Bobbie being a bridesmaid at the simple ceremony, and nothing Bobbie said would dissuade her.

However, when she announced her intention of paying for Bobbie's dress herself, Bobbie put her foot down.

'Oh no, you won't, Viv. I'm relatively wealthy at the moment, as it happens.'

'Good. Although you might have second thoughts when you see the dress I've picked out for you. I found it yesterday and it's just perfect for you, Bobbie.'

Bobbie had to laugh at her. She said, 'Viv, I wonder if Richard realises just what a managing sort of person you are?'

Vivian pulled into a parking spot. 'I told him,' she replied cheerfully. 'He said he adored every little bit of me.'

But once inside the elegant boutique and arrayed in the dress of Vivian's choice, Bobbie had to admit that she couldn't have chosen better herself. The dress itself was quite simple with a high round neck and long sleeves and a plain fitted bodice that emphasised the swell of her breasts and the slimness of her waist. The skirt was full, she found as she twirled in front of the mirror, but as she stood still it settled in graceful folds about her hips. The material was a fine silky knit in a beautiful ivory-beige shade and at the waist there was a small posy of velvet flowers in a delicate shade of green.

Bobbie stared at herself and was amazed at how creamy her skin looked and how green her eyes.

'What do you think, Bobbie?' Vivian asked.

'I . . . I like it,' Bobbie said softly, and then with a chuckle, 'Don't look so worried, Viv. I saw the price tag. It's probably quite crazy to pay so much for a dress I'll wear once a year if I'm lucky, but I'm hooked, I'm afraid.'

'So you should be, Bobbie. You look fantastic in it, love.'

Vivian chose for herself a cream georgette dress with flowing lines that reminded Bobbie of a dress one would have worn to a garden party in a bygone era. It suited Vivian to perfection, and she told her so.

'Do you think Richard will like it, Bobbie?'

Bobbie replied with perfect sincerity, 'If he can take his eyes off you while you're in that dress, I'll be very surprised, Viv.'

Vivian laughed and coloured slightly.

They chose their shoes together and Bobbie settled for a pair of beige suede high-heeled sandals with an ankle strap.

'I just hope I don't break my neck,' she muttered, to the shop assistant's surprise.

It was when they were on their way home that she voiced the problem that was uppermost in her mind. She had been on the point of mentioning it several times to Vivian, but hadn't like to introduce any topic that could dim Vivian's happiness. And she somehow hadn't been able to broach the subject to Rod himself.

But she couldn't prevent herself from saying suddenly as they drove through Kilmore in the gathering dusk, 'Viv, has Rod told you what . . . what will happen to me . . . when you go?'

Vivian shook her head. 'He's being rather mysterious, Bobbie—which as you might have noticed he has a habit of when he's so minded! But as a matter of fact I did ask him last night and he said not to worry, he'd sort it all out.' She broke off and glanced at Bobbie. 'I know how you must feel, but honestly, Bobbie, much as I get annoyed with him sometimes, I do know you can trust him completely. If he says he'll work something out he will. And the last thing he'd do is turf you out, so please don't worry about that.'

Bobbie opened her mouth to reply, but the frown on Vivian's face stopped her and she said instead with a smile, 'Oh well, I guess he'll tell me in his own good time.' And she went on to talk about the wedding as if she didn't have a care in the world.

But the days passed and suddenly it was the eve of

the wedding before he spoke about it, and then only in passing when Vivian had gone to bed and Bobbie was tidying up the lounge before turning in herself.

He looked up from the depths of an armchair where he was reading a book on breeding and said as she straightened the rug, 'By the way, Bobbie, I won't be here tomorrow night. I'm flying up to Sydney for a couple of days after the wedding. Do you think you can manage? We've got no horses nominated for next week, so you can take things a bit easier, and Des Mead will be coming over every day to give you a hand. As a matter of fact, he used to work for me in Sydney, so he knows the ropes.'

Des was the eldest Mead son, a young man of about twenty-three with a passion for trotting.

'Oh,' said Bobbie. 'Yes, I'm sure I can manage with Des to help.'

She waited for him to say more, but he returned to his book and it was only when she said goodnight and started up the staircase that he looked up again.

'By the way, Bobbie, just in case I forget tomorrow,' he grinned, 'I've written out all my instructions and pinned them to the feedroom door. I've detailed exactly how I want each horse worked and there's a phone number there to ring in case you need to get in touch with me.'

'Oh,' she said again. 'All right. Goodnight, Rod.'

' 'Night, Bobbie.'

The wedding went without a hitch. Bobbie looked round the flower-filled room of the old farmhouse as the simple ceremony drew to a close and felt a lump in her throat for several reasons.

It had been a short but beautifully moving service, and the rapt look on both Vivian's and Richard's faces had been enough to move anyone. Even Rod, who had given Vivian away and was now standing beside Bobbie looking incredibly handsome in his dark suit and gleaming white shirt, was touched, she could tell by the intent expression on his face.

And the room itself had never looked lovelier. In between her other chores over the past week Bobbie had scrubbed and polished and all the beautiful old woodwork and copper glowed and shone and reflected the flowers.

Mum would have been so proud, she thought, and winked away a sudden tear. If only it was still mine. . . .

But she pushed these thoughts resolutely away. It was Vivian's day, and nothing should mar it.

And there was no doubt it was a very happy reception that followed and a tribute to Vivian's and Rod's popularity. Several people had flown down from New South Wales for the occasion to swell the ranks of Richard's family and other friends that the Simpsons had made since coming to Victoria.

Champagne corks popped and the exquisite savouries and canapés that the caterers had produced seemed to disappear as fast as they were put out.

Bobbie knew some of the people too and found she herself was the centre of some attraction, which she put down to the new dress and new image she presented. But it wasn't until she was embarking on her second glass of champagne that she had cause to revise that opinion.

Strangely enough it was Mrs Mead who brought it all out in the open. Bobbie had known Mrs Mead all her life and was very fond of her, but at the same time she recognised, as did the whole district, that this kind, motherly woman, who had raised seven children, had one glaring fault. She spoke exactly as she thought, and what was in her mind came out in a generally rambling monologue with no attempt at censorship or even consideration for whose presence she might be in. Her own family had given up years ago trying to cure her of this habit and instead found that her multitude of good points far outweighed this one habit, however disconcerting it could be. And it was a standing joke in the district that if you wanted to hear the unvarnished truth about yourself all you had to do was go along and talk to Mrs Mead.

And so it was that Bobbie was sipping champagne and watching Vivian cut the wedding cake and attending to what was Mrs Mead was saying with only half an ear. Until, that was, Michael Findlay's name cropped up.

'. . . never did go much on him myself. I always thought he was a sly kind of a child, and the rumours he's spreading around the place about you and Rod Simpson simply enforce that, Bobbie. I don't for one minute see you as the type of girl who would have an affair with anyone, and so I shall tell him the very next time I meet him—and anyone else who happens to mention it. So you can count on me, my dear, to help slay this . . . this smear campaign before it gets out of hand. Why, I remember the day as if it were only yesterday when he pinched something and blamed it on Des, which is exactly what I told Mrs Evans in the supermarket the other day when she started talking about you and. . . .'

Bobbie put her half-full glass down carefully on the oak chest beside her and turned to Mrs Mead, only to find that good lady had drifted away and she was staring up into Rod Simpson's grey eyes.

He said with raised eyebrows, 'What's the matter, Bobbie? A second ago you looked as if you'd seen a ghost and now you're all flushed. Too much champagne?' he asked with a quirk to his lips.

She swallowed stiffly. 'Yes,' she said quickly, 'it must be that. Excuse me, will you, I think Viv's gone up to change. I'll go and help her. . . .'

And she walked swiftly away, conscious of his ironic glance.

Once upstairs she put her hands to her hot cheeks and stood stock still in the middle of the passageway.

Oh, I could die! she told herself, but Vivian's voice interrupted these agitated reflections.

'Is that you, Bobbie? I need some help.'

'Coming!' She cleared her throat. 'Coming, Viv,' she called again.

The rest of the wedding passed in a painful blur for Bobbie. She smiled mechanically and said all the right things, she noted with amazement, and she caught the bridal bouquet as everyone applauded. She hugged Vivian tightly and kissed her goodbye, and received an exuberant hug from the bridegroom.

And at the last minute, just as Vivian was about to step into the car, she turned to Bobbie.

'Oh, Bobbie, I nearly forgot to tell you! Rod's arranged. . . .'

Bobbie interrupted swiftly. 'Yes. You better hurry, Viv, you'll miss your plane.'

'Oh, so he told you, Bobbie? I'm so pleased!' And

they clung together for a moment until Richard tooted the horn.

Vivian said hurriedly, 'I told you to trust him, chicken, didn't I? 'Bye for now!'

And they drove away with cheerful waves.

It wasn't long after that the last of the guests departed and the caterers too, leaving the house as clean and tidy as they had found it. Bobbie stood in the middle of the lounge with her hands clasped together anxiously as she listened to Rod moving around upstairs, her mind still in a fearful turmoil. And then his firm tread came on the stairway and she turned away suddenly to stand in front of the window.

'Bobbie?'

'Yes, I'm here,' she said, hoping her voice sounded normal.

He had changed, she saw, into linen sports trousers and a close-fitting polo-necked sweater beneath a tweed jacket.

She couldn't stop herself from letting her gaze rest on him. After all, she told herself, I won't be seeing him again, whatever his plan is.

He had a small leather overnight bag in his hand which he let drop to the floor as he came over to her.

He said, 'The house will seem awfully quiet without Viv. Are you sure you'll be all right on your own? I'm certain Mrs Mead could fit in an extra body.'

'No!' she said hastily, then took a deep breath to steady herself. 'You forget,' she added, 'I'm quite used to it.'

'So you are,' he said with a grin, and touched her cheek lightly with his fingers. 'By the way, did I tell you, you look very lovely in that dress?'

Bobbie looked down at herself quickly to hide the confusion in her eyes.

Rod glanced at his watch. 'I've got to hit the road. Tell you what, while I'm away would you mind giving Viv's room a bit of a going over? Because I'm bringing back a housekeeper with me.' He picked up the case and smiled at her look of bewilderment. 'You'll like her, she used to "do" for Viv and me before Viv left school. It's merely a question of unearthing her and bringing her back, which is one reason for this trip to Sydney. After considerable thought, I decided that even in the cool light of sanity I couldn't stomach the idea of Aunt Victoria.' He dropped a careless arm about her shoulders. 'Don't do anything rash while I'm away, will you, Bobbie?'

And before she could think of a suitable reply he was gone, and she stood and listened to the roar of the car dwindling into the distance.

Bluey whined once and came over to her to lick her hand. She sank down into a chair.

'But what difference does it make, Bluey?' she asked him as she fondled his ears. 'People were talking while Viv was here. A housekeeper won't change anything. These ugly rumours will grow—perhaps could it be I'm giving myself away somehow just in the way I look at him on top of what Mike's spreading around?' And she shivered suddenly at the thought of Rod getting to hear what was being said and, worse, guessing what her real feelings were.

'It's . . . just hopeless, Bluey old son. This time I have to go—we have to go. I should have done it in the first place. Des can manage on his own. He could come and stay if he likes, can't he?' Bluey thumped his tail. 'So it wouldn't be as if I was running out on the job.'

She closed her eyes and leant her head back, unaware of the tears that trickled down her cheeks. 'And it's got to be tonight,' she said half to herself and half to the patient dog. 'Because if I put it off, I won't have the strength to go, I know.'

She never quite knew how she found the will-power to do it, but five minutes later she was upstairs in her bedroom with two suitcases open on the bed and she was packing clothes into them with a mechanical precision.

And when she heard the sound of a car in the drive-way she paused and tried to work out who on earth it could be. Dusk had fallen and she couldn't imagine who would be calling on her at this hour.

She waited for the knocker to sound, but instead, to her intense surprise, she heard the front door opening and closing and then a tread on the stairway.

She froze in the middle of the room with a folded pair of pyjamas in her hands as Bluey jumped off the bed with an eager bark and swung round, to see Rod filling the doorway. She gasped and the pyjamas fell from her nerveless fingers.

He strode into the room and his eyes fell on the suit-cases. Then he cursed fluently before he said to her with coldest look in his eyes,

'Just what the hell do you think you're doing, Bobbie Hallam?'

CHAPTER EIGHT

In her worst nightmare, Bobbie couldn't imagine encountering a more difficult situation.

She licked her lips and said hoarsely, 'Your plane! You'll miss it. . . .'

'Forget about my plane,' he said through gritted teeth and with a savagery that caused her to wince. 'Just answer my question.'

'I . . . well,' she stammered, 'I'm packing.'

'I can see that. It would also appear that you'd planned to run out on me and leave a stable full of horses the minute my back's turned.'

'No!' she cried. 'It's not like that. I was going to get Des to come and stay. He would have managed!'

'But why?' Rod shot at her, and at the same time took her shoulders in a bruising grasp. 'Don't tell me,' he said contemptuously, 'that you're running scared because of Mrs Mead's maundering gossip?'

'You . . . know?' she whispered, and felt a treacherous blush steal up from the base of her throat.

'I've just discovered it,' he said through his teeth. 'I stopped off at the Meads' to give Des some last-minute instructions and she favoured me with what I then realised she'd poured into your ear this afternoon. A whole lot of vicious nonsense. What surprises me,' he added grimly, 'is the fact that I didn't immediately realise that you wouldn't be mature enough to treat it with the contempt it deserves!'

Bobbie stared at him with wide eyes and said with a tremor in her voice, 'But you see, I know what it's like in these country places. Everyone will believe it. I . . . I wondered why they were all so . . . so fascinated this afternoon. Now I know. There's nothing—only one thing I *can* do, and that's go!'

She straightened beneath his hands and tilted her head back with some of her old fighting spirit, then winced as he shook her.

But it was his next words that caused her to do something she had never done in her life before.

He said roughly, 'Oh yes, there is—if that's the case. You can marry me, and that's exactly what we shall be doing as soon as I can arrange it.'

And that was when the room started to rotate before her bewildered eyes and his taut figure began to loom alarmingly over her. She sagged in his arms in a dead faint.

It was Bluey leaning over her, she realised as she came to. He was trying to lick her face. She pushed him aside with trembling hands and tried to sit up, but Rod re-entered the room at that moment with a glass of brandy in his hands and at his sharp command Bluey leapt out of the bed.

He sat down beside her and held the glass to her lips with one hand as he supported her with the other.

'Drink this, Bobbie. It'll make you feel better.'

She took a sip of brandy and lay back with a shuddering sigh. He put the glass down and picked up one of her hands in his.

He said as he massaged her hand gently, 'How do you feel now?'

'Better, thank you,' she whispered with her eyes

closed, and conscious once more of an enormous embarrassment.

'Look at me, Bobbie,' said Rod quietly but insistently.

'Look,' she said in a thread of a voice but with her eyes still tightly shut. 'Please ... you don't have to ... let's just forget about it ...'

'Bobbie!' Her eyes fluttered open at the grim note of warning in his voice. He heaved a sudden sigh, but his eyes never left her face as he said. 'I'm sorry. Sorry for the way I treated you just now. Sorry that you had to hear those ugly rumours. And particularly sorry that you should have been thrown into such a panic. With nowhere to go and no one to turn to—I can imagine how you felt. But you should surely know by now that whatever other failings I have, I do have your best interests at heart.' He paused and traced a pattern on her hand with one finger and appeared to be absorbed in it for a moment. Then he raised his head again and looked directly at her. 'But I'm not sorry about asking you to marry me.' He grinned briefly but humourlessly. 'If you can call what I said a proposal. But I meant it as such and still do. Very much so.'

Bobbie found that a curious dignity came to her aid as she said softly, 'It's ... very kind of you, Rod. And you're right, I should have known better than to just ... just run away. But I couldn't accept your proposal because I know very well that under any other circumstances you would never have made it. Please, will you let me go? I'll be all right. I'm a lot tougher than I look, you know.'

He stood up with a sudden restless movement and crossed to the window to stare out into the dark night.

She waited with bated breath. Finally he turned to her and said abruptly, 'As a matter of fact, it had occurred to me before this—to marry you, I mean. But I hadn't intended to rush into it quite like this. However, in view of the circumstances . . . do you find the idea of me as a husband completely abhorrent, Bobbie?'

'I . . . well,' she stammered, thrown completely off guard by the question, 'that's not the point, is it? I mean, people fall in love—like Viv and Richard did. That's why one gets married, isn't it?'

Rod came back to the bed and sat down and took her hand again. He said with a wry smile that seemed to pierce her heart, 'That is the accepted way these days, but there's a whole lot of evidence to suggest that it's no more, in fact could be even less successful, than the other way.'

She wet her lips and whispered haltingly, 'What other . . . way?'

'Well, take someone like myself. I can't deny that I've knocked around a bit and been pursued as well having done my fair share of pursuing. But I'm conscious now of a need to settle down. In days not so long gone I would have looked around and chosen someone suitable, and not necessarily someone I was wildly in love with.'

Bobbie's fingers trembled suddenly within his and he increased the pressure on her hand as his grey eyes seemed to bore into her own.

He went on. 'Which is not to say that two people who make a contract of this nature can't grow into a very close relationship. In fact, as I said, provided there's no absolute physical revulsion on either side, it would seem that this way has a very good chance of success. And if you were agreeable, while I wouldn't be offering you young love with all its joys and its pain, I would be offering you security and a chance to mature alongside my quite considerable respect for you. You see, I'm prepared to make this a lifetime involvement— commitment, if you like—and I'm fairly certain that with a bit of care and consideration we can nurture something very fine between us. Also, and I don't say this with any pride, but for your own sake as a girl who is blossoming into womanhood it's ... well, the world out there is full of pitfalls, whereas I've already nego-tiated all that, and with a certain wisdom and experi-ence one inevitably acquires along the way, I could make sure *your* first experience of love wouldn't be something to look back on and regret.' He grimaced. 'I know it sounds cynical and—well, whatever you like to think, but it's a fact of life.'

The silence lengthened as Bobbie sought desperately for words and tried to still the urgent pounding of her heart.

Finally Rod said, 'Will you make me a solemn promise, Bobbie?'

She nodded mutely.

'If I leave you here tonight to think this over, you won't run away? I've missed my plane now, but I'll put up overnight at the pub in Kilmore and I'll be back first thing in the morning for your answer.' She stirred and he went on, 'But whatever you decide, even if it's no— I'll sort this problem out somehow. Just ... trust me, Bobbie.'

Bobbie drew back the heavy curtains in her luxury hotel room and looked anxiously out at the weather. It was a typical Melbourne winter day, cold and wet, and she thought ruefully back to an old saying of her mother's—happy the bride that the sun shines on.

'Just my luck to have a wet, grisly day for my wedding day,' she said out loud, and immediately pulled herself up. I've got to get out of the habit of talking aloud, she told herself. Particularly when Bluey's not around.

She glanced at her watch. It was only seven o'clock and she had ordered breakfast at seven-thirty, so she hopped back into bed and snuggled beneath the covers and allowed her mind to roam over the past incredible days. Right back to the morning after the wedding, Vivian's wedding.

Rod had been as good as his word and had returned before she had even gone down to the stables to do the morning feeds. In fact she had bumped into him at the back door. And the mere sight of him had driven all her good intentions and carefully rehearsed speech from her mind, and instead of the polite refusal she had intended to give him she had stuttered and stammered at his look of enquiry and lapsed into a state of complete incoherency.

He had thrust her inside unceremoniously and pushed her into a chair and poured himself a cup of coffee, then said with a glint of amusement in his eyes that did very strange things to her heart, 'Well, Bobbie, are you going to take the plunge and marry me?'

And to her amazement, as she had opened her mouth to say no, but in the very act of forming the word, she had halted and then said gruffly, 'Yes, thank you very much.' And immediately blushed bright scarlet.

His eyes had narrowed slightly as they rested on her

hot face before he said briefly, 'Good girl.' Then he had outlined his plans for the days until the wedding.

Bobbie was still in a state of shock when he delivered her that morning to this same hotel and informed her that he was sending someone round to see her to help her choose her trousseau and that she should not be afraid to put herself completely in this persons' hands because she was a very old friend of his. He had added that he would ring her every day and he hoped to get into town as often as possible until he could arrange the wedding.

Then he had left her, saying, 'You know, Bobbie, I can think of someone who'll be overjoyed at this marriage.'

She had stared at him.

'Yes,' he had said with a smile tugging at his lips, 'Bluey. And don't worry about him while you're here. I'll look after him!'

And it was not long afterwards that Tracey Windham knocked on the door of her room and introduced herself.

Bobbie had been tongue-tied and awkward for a little while because Tracey was the epitome of mature, elegant womanhood. From the top of her shining brown hair to the tips of her fashionable shoes, she exuded sophistication, and yet Bobbie discovered that her eyes were warm and friendly and entirely uncritical.

But it was when Tracey said to her, 'Bobbie, I think you're going to be perfect for Rod,' that she capitulated and allowed herself to respond in the same warm fashion.

And she had seen Tracey every day from then on and

they had had a wonderful time choosing clothes for Bobbie and visiting Tracey's beauty parlour and hairdresser.

It was on the third day of their acquaintance that Bobbie had got to know Tracey's background, almost by accident.

Tracey had said to her as they sipped coffee in the hotel bedroom after an exhausting shopping spree, 'By the way, you haven't told me where you're going for your honeymoon, Bobbie. Is it a secret?'

'Well, as a matter of fact, Tracey,' Bobbie had said unselfconsciously, 'I don't even know if we're going away at all. I haven't seen Rod since he . . . left me here, although we've spoken on the phone.' She had stopped and coloured faintly as she realised how odd it must sound. She had added lamely, 'We're very busy, you see, with the horses . . .'

Tracey had put down her coffee cup with a thoughtful expression on her face. 'Bobbie,' she had said slowly, 'is there anything you'd like to tell me? I'm quite a bit older than you are, you know,' she had added with a rueful grin, 'and I do know Rod very well—I suppose he's told you all about me?'

Bobbie shook her head. 'No. Only that you're a very good friend.'

Tracey's sigh had been exasperated. 'I sometimes wonder about men and how their minds work!' And she had grown thoughtful again as she had said slowly, 'Bobbie, Rod and I were . . . well, more than good friends, I guess you could say. In fact we were engaged once.'

Bobbie had stiffened.

Tracey had gone on with a funny little smile on her

face, 'We were . . . crazy about each other, but—well,
you see I'm—how can I put it—not a horsey person, if
you know what I mean? In fact I'm terrified of horses.
And as we grew closer, the greater the strain became.
And every time I saw Rod driving in a race, the more of
a nervous wreck I became until the day I begged and
pleaded with him to give it up. But even while I was
doing it I was hating myself, because I knew it was his
life.' She'd looked down at her hands and said slowly,
'We were both very young and what followed seemed
. . . agonising, but I couldn't change myself and neither
could he. So we agreed to . . . to part.'

Bobbie had found she was quite bereft of words.

Tracey had continued wryly. 'At the time I felt like
. . . well, like drowning myself or doing something
crazy, but time does heal, as they say, and one day I
met Steve Windham and fell in love with him and have
been very happily married to him ever since. You'll
meet him one day because, strange as it may seem, he
and Rod are good friends, but he's overseas on business at present. And up until now I've only had one
regret—that Rod hasn't found someone himself, because I'm still conscious, even though I know it would
never have worked for us, that I inflicted some sort of a
scar on him. Oh, I don't kid myself that he still hankers
for me, but I have wondered if the experience hasn't . . .
hasn't left him, sort of unwilling to really commit himself again.'

Bobbie had desperately wanted to break the silence
that had followed, but had found herself quite unable
to.

And finally Tracey had said, 'That's why I was so
happy to hear about you Bobbie and—well, all I'd like

to say is this. If you ever feel you need someone to confide in, please think of me. Because I'd be more than willing to help both of you if ever I could.'

And Bobbie had been very tempted to tell Tracey the whole story, but somehow she had been unable to formulate the words. And yet it was as if some unspoken contact had been established between them which lessened the growing feeling of isolation that had been threatening her.

A knock on the door brought her back to the present. She ate her breakfast, and then because she had nothing else to do until Tracey arrived to collect her for the wedding which was to be held at ten o'clock, she dressed herself with great care in the dress she had bought for Vivian's wedding only a week ago, never dreaming that she would be wearing it to her own wedding.

And she was happy when Tracey's knock sounded on the door half an hour earlier than planned because she found herself suddenly assailed by the most peculiar sensation in the pit of her stomach—a sensation she had not experienced since the first time a horse had bolted with her.

She pulled open the door eagerly, then took an uncertain step backwards. For it was not Tracey but Marianne Hunter who stood there.

Marianne looked her up and down and said, 'Well, aren't you going to invite me in, Bobbie?'

'I . . . I. . . .' Bobbie stammered, but Marianne sauntered past her and sat herself down in one of the armchairs. She crossed her legs and drew out a cigarette.

'How's the bride-to-be?' she asked casually. 'I must say you're a dark horse, Bobbie.'

'Who ... who told you I was here?' Bobbie asked stiffly.

'Why, Rod, of course! Who did you think it would be?' Marianne blew out a cloud of smoke and regarded Bobbie through half-closed eyes as she said, 'Surely you're not so naïve as to believe that this marriage is going to change anything between Rod and myself, Bobbie?' She chuckled suddenly. 'As a matter of fact I'm sure he's half-way to regretting it already, but being something of an obstinate creature, he'll go through with it—for the time being, anyway.'

'What ... what do you mean?' Bobbie whispered.

'I mean, dear Bobbie, that Rod and I had a disagreement, such a silly one too, but he got rather furious and he made some rather rash statements.' Marianne shrugged and regarded the tip of her cigarette for a moment. Then she raised her cold blue eyes to Bobbie's face and said baldly, 'He told me that he was going to marry the first willing female he could find. I'm afraid I have a bit of a temper too and I told him he had my blessing. And that's how he came to propose to you—in a fit of temper, I suppose you could say. Which incidentally, as I've remarked, he's already beginning to regret. My dear, I give you six months at the most with him. Because he won't be able to stay away from me any longer—if he makes it for that long!' She stubbed out her cigarette and stood up with a sinuous grace. 'After all,' she murmured with a lingering glance at herself in the mirror and then a flicking glance for Bobbie, 'while you look perfectly sweet, my pet, in that dress, you mustn't forget that Rod is a very sophisticated man.'

And she strolled towards the door, but paused with

her hand on the handle to say, 'Just in case you doubt any of this why don't you ask him why he had dinner with me last night and for that matter, the night before?'

The door closed gently behind her.

Bobbie stood in the centre of the room as if frozen like a statue, unable to halt the awful spreading numbness that seemed to envelope her and was so much worse than the sensation of butterflies she had had before.

Another knock sounded on the door, but she was still unable to move, unable to speak, and when Tracey let herself into the room it was to find her staring blindly before her with a pathetically white, frightened face.

She asked as she hurried over to her, 'What is it, Bobbie? What's the matter?'

'I . . . I . . . Tracey!' Bobbie exclaimed in sudden desperation, 'I can't go through with this. You'll have to tell Rod for me!'

'Bobbie, sit down, will you,' Tracey said firmly, and pushed her into a chair. She reached for the phone and ordered two brandies. Then she said humorously, 'It's a bit early, I don't know what they'll think, but you look as if you could do with one.' She sat down herself on the arm of the chair and took one of Bobbie's hands in hers. 'Now tell me about it, love. You know, I think all brides go through some form of nerves, but you mustn't be afraid of Rod, Bobbie. He would never do anything to hurt you.'

'It's not that, Tracey.' Bobbie turned to her urgently. 'I always knew he didn't love me, but I was prepared to take the risk all the same. Now . . . I know now that not only doesn't he love me but he's very much in love with someone else. and he's only marrying me in a fit of pique!'

Tracey's eyes narrowed and she said slowly, 'Bobbie, that doesn't sound like the Rod I know, and I know him well, as I told you, but—tell me, was that Marianne Hunter I saw leaving the hotel just as I arrived?'

'Yes,' Bobbie whispered. 'She came to see me.'

'Oh, Bobbie!' Tracey put an arm about her shoulders and said with uncharacteristic force, 'That . . . woman! She—well, never mind. Look. . . .' She broke off as the waiter knocked and entered with the two drinks.

Bobbie took a sip of hers as Tracey continued, 'Look, Bobbie, if Rod had wanted to marry Marianne he could have done it any time these past couple of years. And if anyone's suffering from a fit of pique, she is. Believe me! I only wish Viv was here to tell you all about her.'

Bobbie was forced to grin weakly at the thought of Vivian's opinion of Marianne Hunter. But she sobered at Tracey's next words.

'And why are you so sure he doesn't love you, Bobbie?'

'Because . . . because he told me so,' she said gruffly.

Tracey was silent for a moment before she said, 'Bobbie, I don't pretend to understand all this, but just from the way you were the night he took us to dinner— well, I got the impression that you're very much in love with him.'

Bobbie hesitated and then nodded, as two tears trickled slowly down her cheeks.

Well then, love, take your courage in your two hands and go forward to your wedding this morning with all your usual determination and spirit—Rod's told me all about that, by the way, your grit and pluck—and make the very best of it that you can!'

Which was precisely what Bobbie did that morning, with Tracey by her side to lend moral support, and as they came out of the register office, the sun actually broke through the clouds and shone briefly. But all the time, and particularly when she looked at the tall, handsome, wordly man standing beside her, she was conscious of a feeling akin to panic. And all the time, like an unsteady refrain, the thought ran through her mind that perhaps Marianne had been right. Because it just didn't seem possible that Rod Simpson could be marrying Bobbie Hallam.

And then she was no longer Bobbie Hallam, but Roberta Simpson, and she had a gold band on her left hand to prove it.

Together with Tracey they had lunch at an exclusive restaurant and neither Rod nor Tracey seemed to notice that she was rather quiet and unusually flushed.

It was one-thirty when Tracey left them and soon they were in the sleek grey sports car and headed for home. Once he had negotiated the city traffic, Rod pulled the car up and turned to her.

'Bobbie,' he said as he slid his arm along the back of her seat and loosened his tie with his other hand.

'Yes?'

He smiled suddenly and said softly, 'Don't look so frightened, Bobbie, I'm not going to eat you. Although in that dress you look good enough to eat.' His free hand came up and he traced the line of her jaw with gentle fingers. 'You know,' he said, suddenly serious, 'I was going to ask you if you minded very much not having a honeymoon—just yet anyway. But. . . .'

She interrupted, 'I don't mind, Rod, really. I know how difficult it is to get away with horses. I'm honestly very happy just to be going home.'

'Well, if you're sure?'

She nodded.

He took his fingers from her face and pulled something out of his pocket. 'I wanted to give you this when we were alone,' he said as he opened the cream velvet box.

Bobbie gasped, for in his hand lay a magnificent emerald and diamond engagement ring.

Rod said as he slid it on to her nerveless left hand, 'As soon as I saw it, I knew it had to be yours, because it matches your eyes.'

'Oh, Rod,' she said finally when she was able to speak, 'it's beautiful! Too beautiful for me. I. . . .'

'That's a matter of opinion, Bobbie,' he said with a wry grin. 'Anyhow, it's yours now.' And he bent his head and kissed her lightly on the lips.

CHAPTER NINE

BLUEY was beside himself with joy when Bobbie stepped out of the car, and Rod said laughingly, 'I told you so. Although he might not be quite so happy tonight when he discovers he's been ousted from your bed!'

He advanced towards her and picked her up in his arms before she quite realised what he was about, and said with another grin, 'It's just as well you're a light-weight, Bobbie, because this seems to be becoming quite a habit.' He carried her over the doorstep and set her down gently in the middle of the lounge room. 'Welcome home, Mrs Simpson,' he said gently.

She stood for a moment in the circle of his arms, prey once again to all those sensations any close contact with him brought on, the accelerated heartbeat and weakness of her limbs, but this time there was a difference. She was conscious of an overwhelming urge to touch him, to wind her arms round his neck and offer her mouth to his kiss, but at the same time an agony of shyness held her in its grip, coupled with a terrible fear of making a fool of herself, and so she stood unmoving until his arms dropped away and he said lightly,

'Why don't you get yourself unpacked, Bobbie? I think I'll go down and check on the horses. By the way, I've employed Des on a permanent part-time basis to help us out. There are several big races coming up soon, so we'll be flat out. I'm giving Morningtown his first start at Moonee Valley in about a month's time. I should have a surprise for you by then, by the way, Bobbie.'

'Oh,' she said, relieved that he had moved away but at the same time unhappy with herself. 'What . . . what is it?'

'If I told you now, it wouldn't be a surprise, would it?' he said quizzically. 'I'm afraid you'll have to wait and see.' And with a laughing look over his shoulder he disappeared through the back door.

Bobbie sat down slowly and looked around her as if she was seeing the familiar room through new eyes. Unpack, he'd said, she thought. And that brings me slap bang up against the problem I've been too petrified to even contemplate. Where should I unpack? Are we going to share a room right from the beginning? Her mind flew to the double bed that her parents had shared in what had subsequently become Vivian's bedroom, and Rod's earlier words came back to her. . . . 'when he discovers he's been ousted from your bed'.

'That's what he does mean, Bluey,' she said out loud, and forced herself to continue, 'that we share not only a room but a bed tonight.' Her cheeks burned at the awesome, unbelievable thought, and she stood up restlessly and moved aimlessly about the room until her eyes rested on a small pile of unopened mail on the bureau.

On the top of the pile was a large typewritten envelope, addressed to her. She frowned for a moment as she stopped pacing and picked it up. She wasn't the recipient of much mail, other than bills, normally, and this didn't look like a bill. She was still frowning as her fingers tore open the envelope and pulled out a piece of thin cardboard that was folded in half. She unfolded the cardboard gingerly, then put out a hand to steady herself against the bureau as six glossy photographs fluttered to the floor. One glimpse had been enough to tell her what they were, but after a moment she forced herself to pick them up and study each one in turn. There was no note included by way of explanation, but in fact each photograph was self-explanatory and she had no doubt who had sent them to her.

And although each background was different, the main subjects were the same: Rod and Marianne dancing cheek to cheek or smiling into each other's eyes. But perhaps the unkindest one of all was of Marianne smiling straight at the camera and Rod captured with his eyes on her beautiful face and an expression of undeniable pride in them.

The small sigh she heard was her own, Bobbie realised as she packed the photos sadly back into the envelope, and all at once she knew what she had to do.

'I can't . . . I just can't make do with the scraps of his affection,' she told Bluey. 'It's really a matter of pride after all, old son. It somehow seems as if I'm grovelling, ready to take him on any terms at all, and I can't understand why I didn't see it sooner. Surely it's better to have some self-respect left, even if it makes me thoroughly miserable?' Bluey thumped his tail on the floor. 'Which doesn't mean to say, old son,' she continued, 'that I'm giving up just yet. But I must admit she's won the first round. Which means, from your point of view, Bluey, that we'll be back to square one tonight, with you on the foot of my own bed after all tonight. Although I'm not quite sure how on earth I'm going to explain it to him. . . .'

But in the end she found she didn't have to explain anything, and afterwards she wished vehemently that she only could have.

By some superhuman effort she managed to appear

normal throughout the rest of that long, long day. And it wasn't until after they had had dinner, during which Rod had opened a bottle of wine, that he had gone upstairs and discovered none of Bobbie's things in the main bedroom.

She had prepared herself for his scorn or even anger, but he had merely come down again with a thoughtful expression on his face and said, 'Sit down, Bobbie, will you. It appears we have something to discuss. Forget about the dishes.'

And he propelled her towards an armchair and then busied himself pouring them each another glass of wine and putting another log on the fire. Finally he sat down in the chair opposite her, by which time she was a bundle of nerves and clutching the stem of her wine-glass tightly.

'Bobbie,' his grey eyes glinted at her across the intervening space, 'it seems I might have miscalculated slightly.' His eyes fell on her white knuckles and narrowed, and he reached across and prised her fingers open, removed the glass from her grasp and set it down on the coffee table.

He said in a gentler tone, 'Bobbie, there are two ways of going about . . . our marriage, and I'm afraid I rather unthinkingly opted for the most obvious, perhaps. I had thought that you weren't entirely—what's the word—unmoved by me.'

She blushed painfully and hoped devoutly that the warm firelight provided her with a camouflage.

He went on soberly, 'And that you would be willing to consummate our marriage here, tonight. I'm afraid,' he looked down at his own glass and swirled the golden liquid in it gently, 'this was obviously a misconception

on my part, and perhaps a rather unthinking one, I realise now.' He looked across at her. 'Look at me,
Bobbie,' he commanded quietly. She met his eyes unwillingly and he went on, 'I realise now that that isn't
your plan.' He waited, and finally she nodded uncertainly.

'All right,' he said in the same even tone and then
with a ghost of a smile, 'don't look so stricken, Bobbie.
I acept, now, your point of view, and perhaps it should
have occurred to me earlier. You're very young and I
suppose it's perfectly natural to want some sort of a
courting period before you're expected to jump into bed
with someone.' He sat forward. 'I also realise that our
main problem is a lack of communication on any subject other than horses.' He grinned suddenly and wryly
as he said, 'I have no doubt, especially after tonight,
that that's the only subject where you're prepared to
trust and accept my views.'

Bobbie winced inwardly and couldn't help thinking
to herself that if he was so contained about it all, even
prepared to laugh about it, it could only be because it
didn't really matter a great deal to him one way or the
other. And she wished suddenly that instead he would
be furiously angry with her—even to the point of
making her go to bed with him—and thought immediately that it was probably the silliest wish she had
ever had in her life.

He went on, 'In the interests of joint communication
perhaps I should say that my owwn feelings on the subject are that now you've taken one plunge, you would
be wise to take the next. You know, Bobbie, very often
these great decisions one is forced to make and one
spends so much time agonising over—very often, when

you look back on them, you can't help wondering what all the fuss was about.'

She moved restlessly in the chair.

Rod stared at her as if trying to read her mind and she thought wildly, how could he possibly know what I want if I don't know myself? Ten minutes ago I was quite resolved, but now. . . .'

And she noted that his voice was a fraction cooler as he said, 'Anyway, whatever the reason is, you can relax for the time being. I have no intention of playing the role of the frustrated husband and demanding my conjugal rights tonight. We'll call a truce for a period and take a little time to get to know each other better.' He smiled, but with a trace of irony. 'Perhaps we did put the cart before the horse, so we'll have our period of "courting" now.'

He drained the wine in his glass and put it carefully down on the table, and Bobbie could only stare at him helplessly with wide eyes as he said, 'But it will lead to the same thing one day, Bobbie, and not in the too-distant future, my sweet innocent, so it might be a good thing if you got used to the idea, because I never intended this to be a marriage in name only and I'm only suggesting this—period—in deference to the fact that you're very young and unsophisticated and could be rather frightened.'

If only he hadn't used . . . used that word, Bobbie thought as she sobbed into her pillow some time later. I know I'm not sophisticated, but that doesn't prevent me from feeling very . . . well, very much like a woman when he's around. Why does everybody keep telling me this? I'm quite a different person now from the Bobbie Hallam who sat by the roadside and cried because she had a flat tyre. She sat up and thought rebelliously, what is sophistication anyway? Does it mean being vicious like Marianne is? And with a quick movement she slipped off the bed and whisked her nightgown over her head in a defiant gesture and stared at herself in the long mirror.

It was the first time in her life that she had taken a long critical look at herself like this, and she tried to visualise the soft curves of her body, with its pale tender skin and faint dusting of freckles like a golden bloom, through Rod's eyes. And she thought almost hysterically to herself, I don't really look like a scrubby tomboy when I'm naked. And I certainly don't feel like one any more. And she wondered, as she stood there, what it would feel like to have his lean strong hands touch her bare skin. . . .'

But the thought was too much for her and she grabbed her nightgown and pulled it on again, then jumped back into bed and pulled the covers right up to her chin. He's right, she told herself. It's not only Marianne, it's also because I'm—more than a little scared, not only of him, but of this new me.

And her last waking thoughts were, if only . . . if only he could say he loved me, then I wouldn't be so nervous . . . of so many things. Of him, of myself, and the fact that in my supreme unsophistication I might do or seem silly. . . .

If the next few weeks brought her pain and pleasure in roughly equal proportions, she also learnt several facts of life. For example, while rumour-mongers had had a field day with little Bobbie Hallam, they were not quite so brave when faced with Rod Simpson, and Bobbie

found that instead of the speculation she had expected
to be treated with when the surprised district learnt of
their marriage, she was suddenly the object of much
almost obsequious attention even from those whom she
knew, from long association with them, would have
been among the first to have been critical of her earlier.

And at every race meeting she attended with Rod, she
found they were always the centre of an admiring
throng. She didn't deceive herself that this was a tribute
to herself in any way but came simply as a result of her
connection with two almost legendary figures. Rod
Simpson and Morningtown. And quite often she had to
pinch herself figuratively, to assure herself that this was
no dream. She might be a wife in name only—as yet—
but to the rest of the world she was inextricably bound
to this man whom many looked upon as an idol, and
his equally famous horse.

And it was to Morningtown that she owed the fact
that she hadn't broken down under the almost intoler-
able strain of it all. Because between the two of them
there was an ever-growing bond of affection and although Bobbie knew that there was one step, one hand
that the horse looked to above all and it would always
be Rod's hand, Rod's voice, all the same the spirited,
intelligent stallion was accepting her more and more.
And whenever things got too much for her, she had got
into the habit of going down to the stables and taking
up a brush and grooming him and talking to him until
she had worked off her blues.

She was quite indignant when Rod twitted her about
it one day.

He said with that faint note of mockery in his voice,
'I wonder if Morningtown and Bluey realise how privi-
leged they are?'

'What do you mean?'

'I mean that you talk to them far more than you talk to me. Or anyone else for that matter.'

She said ruefully, 'I guess I got into the habit of talking out aloud to Bluey after my parents died and I was alone much of the time.' She added with a faint touch of belligerence, 'I suppose you think it's a sign of instability.'

'I didn't say that,' Rod shrugged. 'As a matter of fact I think it's a sign of sanity. If you're on your own, better to talk to a dog than not talk at all. But may I point out, you're no longer on your own. And while you may have reservations about loving, honouring and cherishing me, there's no reason on earth why you shouldn't talk to me. You might—might even find it helps you along the path, obviously a boulder-strewn one, towards achieving those other . . . things.'

She flinched inwardly, but refused to allow it to show in her face. For as the days had progressed she had discovered that Rod had been right about taking the plunge, as he had put it that fateful night of their wedding. Because instead of finding herself more and more at ease with him as she had hoped and closer to weaning him away from Marianne and even coming to love her, instead of this, she found that day by day she became more tongue-tied, more gauche and less able to communicate with him. And she knew miserably that there was one way to end this agony for herself, but she could not, despite her innermost yearnings, find the way to take that step that would bring her to his bed.

She kept telling herself that it was far better not to give herself away because if Rod did ever turn to Marianne, she would have less to regret, less to lose, but even this line of thought wavered as she saw his patient, even gentle manner with her change and become tinged with irony, shot through with a growing although as yet tightly leashed impatience.

And she knew, even more miserably, that if he was so minded, and she still felt she had good cause to believe he was, it wouldn't be long before he sought Marianne out, if he had not already done so.

They had three horses in at Kilmore that disastrous Monday, and from the very outset it was obvious it was going to be a day that kept going wrong.

They both overslept, owing perhaps to the biting cold weather, and it wasn't until Des knocked loudly on the door that they awoke. From then on it was a race against time, and Bobbie discovered that although Rod rarely exhibited any sign of a temper, when he did, he did it with a bitter sarcasm, and it wasn't long before she and Des were both wilting under the lash of his tongue.

But it was the discovery that Des was to drive Best Dressed in a race that Rod had one of his own horses starting that caused Bobbie to lose her temper.

Des had already left with the truck when Bobbie made the discovery, and it was only because Rod told her sharply not to worry to take her gear that she discovered it before they left home.

'What do you mean?' she demanded.

'Just what I said. Are you ready now, because if you're not I'll have to leave without you.' And he stood with his hand on the front door.

But Bobbie suddenly felt goaded beyond endurance and she said tightly, 'No, I am not ready—and you're not going anywhere just yet until you explain yourself.'

'And just how do you propose to prevent me?' he asked acidly.

'Well, as a matter of fact I happen to have both sets of car keys on me. If you recall, you asked me to take your car into town yesterday to have it filled up. So you can just stop and explain to me why I shouldn't take my gear.'

'Very well,' he said on a note of cold anger. 'Because Des is driving Best Dressed today.'

'What!'

'You heard me, Bobbie.'

'But why?' she demanded furiously. 'And who are you to decide that?'

She took a step backwards as he loomed threateningly over and said through his teeth,

'Because I'm your husband—that's why I'm entitled to make the decision, and that's why I don't want you driving in the same race as me. In fact, I don't want you driving at all from now on. It's a ridiculous situation at the best of times, but worse for us to drive in the same field. So you can pack your colours away in mothballs, Bobbie.'

'I'll do no such thing!' she hissed at him. 'And you can't make me. I'm driving that horse today whether you like it or not. You ... you wonder that we can't communicate, and yet you do a thing like this without even consulting me!'

Rod said contemptuously, 'What good would it have done to discuss it with you? You would have felt exactly the same, and in any case there's no ground for discussion, so don't waste your breath arguing with me.'

Which so incensed Bobbie that she raised her hand with the intention of hitting him, but the next few moments proved to her what an unwise reaction this was. For he swept her off her feet, and as she struggled feebly he marched out to the car and deposited her in it and slammed the door on her. Then he strode back to the front door, slammed it closed, then joined her in the car.

'Now,' he said roughly, 'hand over those keys, my little wildcat wife, or you might find you've precipitated more than you can handle.'

She glared at him fiercely, 'You . . . you. . . .!'

'Hand them over, Bobbie,' he rapped out, 'or you'll be sorry!'

She was conscious suddenly of her breast rising and falling rapidly and her burning cheeks and the fact that his mocking grey gaze was roaming over her—and a trembling weakness invaded her limbs at the look in his eyes.

'Here,' she whispered, and plunged her hand into her pocket and drew out the keys.

'Thank you.' He took them from her and the touch of his hand seemed to burn her. She jerked her fingers away and blushed scarlet at the same time.

Rod's eyes narrowed and he said on a more even note, as he turned away, 'You know, Bobbie, I'm beginning to think I made a rather drastic error the day we were married—or rather the first night of our marriage. If I'd done what I wanted to do we wouldn't be going through this little drama right now. And the more I think about it the more convinced I am.' She shivered at the steely note that entered his voice. 'So take warning, my innocent, because I'm giving you fair notice that our period of courtship is drawing to a close.'

And if that wasn't enough, Bobbie felt as she sat miserably on the fence at the track and watched Rod win two races and run second to Best Dressed in the third, the sight of Marianne was.

She'd just better keep away from me, she thought rebelliously, or I might ... well, I don't know what I would do, but it could be something awful.

But Marianne didn't approach her and she didn't see her with Rod, although they could have been together while Bobbie was washing the horses down. But she did see Marianne talking to Michael Findlay, of all people, and she couldn't help pausing and wondering what on earth they would have to talk about. And she found herself shivering slightly at the thought of the combined venom the two of them represented.

Rod wasn't talkative on the drive home, but she gathered that some of his bad temper had been dispersed, if not towards herself, at least towards the world in general. In fact he was whistling softly as they drove into Greentree Farm and he said quite kindly,

'Don't bother to come down, Bobbie. We can manage. Why don't you start tea? And build up the fire.'

Bobbie did as she was bid, and it was while she was preparing the meal that some strange whim took possession of her; she went upstairs and had a warm shower, then changed into one of her new dresses that Tracey had helped her choose. It was a full-length dress in a fine russet-coloured wool that toned with her hair and had a drawstring neckline and long, full sleeves. She brushed her hair till it shone and applied just a touch of make-up as Vivian and Tracey had taught her.

But when she stood back and surveyed herself in the mirror she was suddenly tempted to rip the dress off and seek refuge once more in her jeans. It took some will-power to resist this cowardly impulse, and then it was too late, because Rod had come in, and the surprised look he threw her through her open doorway on his way to his bedroom steeled her, and with a final pat to her hair, she made her way downstairs and started to set the table.

Rod was whistling again as he came down, and she caught her breath at the sight of him, fresh from the shower and dressed casually in a white open-necked silk shirt and matching grey trousers and sweater. And all the way through the meal she found she was infinitely disturbed by the strong brown column of his neck as it rose from the snowy white shirt and the glint in his quizzical grey eyes that were, thank goodness, now less cold when they rested on her.

Finally the last dish was dried and put away and she set a cup of coffee beside him as he sat in front of the fire and sat down herself.

They sipped their coffee in silence for several minutes and Bobbie found that the tensions of the day began to seep away. She glanced round the room, now shadowed and dim beyond the reach of the warm firelight, and for a moment she was transported back to the days of peace and security before her parents had been killed. Then her eyes came to rest on Rod as he stared pensively into the fire. If only . . . if only this homely scene was for real, she mused. If only I was a beloved wife and not merely someone 'suitable'. Someone second best. . . .

She stirred suddenly as she realised Rod had lifted his head and was returning her gaze.

'Penny for your thoughts, Bobbie?' he asked quietly.

'I'm afraid they're not even worth that,' she said with a catch in her voice.

'You're a funny girl, Bobbie. I don't think I've ever met anyone quite like you before.' He paused and added with a grin. 'You look very fetching in that dress. Did you put it on for my benefit?'

'I . . . I guess so.' She found she was stammering.

He passed a hand through his thick brown hair and said wryly, 'Does that mean you've forgiven me for being such a grouch today?'

'. . . Yes,' she said gruffly after a moment. 'I know what race days are like. Dad used to be exactly the same.'

Rod's eyes searched her face before he said lightly, 'Would that it were only race days that were problematical.' He stood up and drew her to her feet and held both her hands in his. 'Bobbie, if you don't hate me and you do trust me, shall we put an end to this farce and start our real marriage—now?'

Her heart leaped into her throat as she stood captured not only by his lean strong hands but by the magnetic force of him that seemed to enmesh her whichever way she turned.

He said very quietly, but she noticed unthinkingly that a pulse throbbed in his jaw, 'Believe me, Bobbie, I'll be as gentle as I know how.' He released one of her hands and traced the line of her cheek with his fingers. 'And you might even find,' he added with a glint in his eyes, 'that what seems now like an enormous step is really what you've wanted all along.'

She found she couldn't argue with this, and she didn't resist as his arms went round her and he lowered his head to kiss her very gently on the lips.

But what started as a gentle kiss soon grew into a wild, passionate one, and for the first time she found the shell that she had built around herself crumbling until with his name on her lips she stood on tiptoe and wound her arms round his neck.

And then, she wasn't quite sure how, but she found herself lying in his lap responding to his kisses with an ardour she hadn't thought herself capable of. And when his sure fingers found the drawstring to the neck of her dress she didn't object, not even when he lifted his head and grinned at her with a tinge of surprised irony in his eyes.

He murmured, 'You don't ever do anything by half measures, do you, Bobbie?'

A tide of warm colour rose up from the base of her throat, as much from his words as the feel of his exploring hand now cupping her breast and very gently roaming across her nipples. The wide-eyed look she gave him was almost a plea for reassurance, and he responded with a sudden look of concern, almost, then a strange, enigmatic expression crossed his face and he tightened his grasp round her shoulders and he laid his head on hers and said very quietly into her hair, 'You remind me of a perfect rosebud just starting to unfurl to greet the sun. And I'm very honoured to be that sun . . .'

But the rest of his words were drowned, because the telephone chose that moment to shrill impatiently across the room. And despite herself Bobbie couldn't prevent herself from stiffening slightly beneath his hands as the sound of the jangling bell cut across her taut nerves.

Rod's grin was rueful as his grip on her slackened and he swore mildly.

'I'll . . . get it,' she said, and scrambled up hastily.

'Tell whoever it is to go to the devil, will you, Bobbie. I'm not home to the telephone right now.' He lay sprawled back in the chair and she was conscious of his intent gaze on her as she crossed the room and the look in his eyes that made her falter and tremble.

But the phone kept ringing.

She picked it up and cleared her throat. 'Hello.'

'Bobbie, is that you, pet? It's Marianne here. I didn't get a chance to talk to you today, did I?' A throaty chuckle came down the line. 'Never mind, I did speak to Rod. By the way, did you get those photos?'

'I . . . yes,' said Bobbie through suddenly stiff lips.

'What did you think of them, Bobbie? Or perhaps I shouldn't ask that. No, probably not,' said Marianne, and chuckled again. 'Be a love and put Rod on, will you? He told me he was going up country for a few days and it so happens I'm going on a trip in the same direction. I just wanted to see whether he'd decided to leave tomorrow or the next day. There seemed to be some doubt. . . .'

Bobbie cut across the flow of words. 'He's here, I'll get him,' she said baldly, and took the phone from her ear.

Rod was standing beside her now and he took the proffered receiver with a look of enquiry.

Bobbie said quietly, 'It's for you. And I think I'll go to bed now. Goodnight, Rod.'

She turned away resolutely and walked towards the staircase with her head held high. But something prompted her to peep over her shoulder once as she climbed the stairs, and it was to see him still holding the receiver at arm's length and staring up at her, and she couldn't prevent a small shiver at the look in his eyes.

CHAPTER TEN

BOBBIE closed her bedroom door firmly enough, and with the precision of a mechanical doll she undressed and got into one of her high-necked, long-sleeved winter nightgowns. She removed her make-up meticulously, cleaned her teeth and brushed her hair, then she moved quietly about the room, tidying up as her mother had trained her, and with a last lingering glance around, she folded back her bedcover neatly and climbed into bed.

She was just reaching out to switch off the beside light when she heard Rod's footsteps in the passageway and she stayed poised as she was as the door swung open before her mesmerised eyes.

'Don't,' he said curtly, and she obediently removed her hand from the lamp.

He advanced a few paces into the room and looked around at the pretty, girlish bedroom. Then his eyes came back to rest on her, taking in the high, frilly collar and concealing folds of her nightgown, her hands clasped loosely on the embroidered sheet and finally, with a look of cold insolence, to her face.

He pushed his hands deep into his pockets and said almost casually, 'A pretty picture, Bobbie, but not quite in keeping with the one you presented to me downstairs such a short time ago. Tell me, what's brought on the change?'

She didn't asnwer but kept her eyes steadily on him until he continued on a more cutting note, 'Is this virginal display calculated to impress on me that you don't approve of Marianne? Because if that's so, I knew that a long time ago, but I'd like to say just one thing. I married you, not her, and I don't intend to spend the rest of my life defending myself on this subject.'

The silence grew as he waited for her reply, but she sat as still as a statue, seeing with agonised eyes not him but those glossy photographs that were even now nestling in one of her bureau drawers as Marianne's words drummed through her brain. 'He's taking a trip up country . . .' But he didn't see fit to tell me about it, she thought, and felt the tears welling up.

'Bobbie!'

She came back with a start and cowered back as he loomed over her and jerked her to her knees with impatient hands.

. He said through his teeth on an impatient breath, 'All right! I've tried the kid glove approach, but now it's time to see if this is how you prefer to be treated.'

And with a world of contempt in his eyes he pushed her down on the bed as if she was a limp rag doll and his strong fingers fumbled with the tiny buttons at her throat, then with an impatient sound he ripped the front of her nightgown apart and he was on the bed beside her, his lips like a trail of fire as they moved punishingly from her slender white throat down to her breasts.

She struggled, desperately afraid of him and conscious of an even greater fear—that her body would betray her as it had downstairs. Because she knew that if she gave in to him now she would be forever enslaved, and she shuddered at the thought of the pain that Rod and Marianne could inflict on her at will.

It was this shudder that seem to cause him to

pause, and raise his head to stare narrowly into her agonised eyes.

It was a long, searching look and when he sat up finally she thought she could die at the cold mockery in his voice as he said, 'Very well, my determined little virgin, I get the message.'

He stood up and watched her as her hands came up and she pulled the edges of her torn nightgown together, her eyes never leaving his face, but her fingers stilled as he laughed sardonically.

'Oh yes,' he drawled, 'it's getting clearer every minute. You know, Bobbie, I didn't believe it of you, but now I'm forced to. You only married me for one reason, didn't you?'

She stared.

'One reason,' he said again very softly. 'To be able to keep this farm. That's the only thing that means anything to you, isn't it? But I must tell you,' he went on with a frightening menace in his voice, 'you can't have one without the other, Bobbie. And the sooner you realise it, the less ... painful it will be for you. No,' he shook his head as she jerked upright, 'I don't mean tonight, my *sweet* wife. I'm afraid my ardour has cooled, you might say, at the realisation of your utter materialism.' He laughed again coldly as he turned to the door. 'But one day soon,' he said lazily over his shoulder, 'it's going to give me great pleasure to teach you a lesson, Bobbie Hallam.'

'Rod!'

But with a mocking salute he closed the door, and she was left to stare at it with horrified eyes as she heard his footsteps retreat down the passage.

Bobbie was heavy-eyed when she came down the next morning after tossing and turning for most of the night and finally falling heavily asleep in the early hours of the cold, grey dawn.

Rod was at the breakfast table drinking coffee, which told her that he had already had a session with the horses, and a glance at the table showed that Des had done likewise. His empty coffee cup and toast plate were still in evidence.

At the sight of Rod, a slow colour crept across her cheeks and she fought an insane desire to scramble upstairs again as fast as she could.

He flicked her an ironic glance as she walked over to the stove and said derisively, 'Good morning, madam wife.'

Bobbie squared her shoulders as she poured her coffee and took it over to the table to join him. Somehow or other she had to get through to him this morning.

But the words died on her lips as his grey eyes rested on the faint violet shadows beneath her eyes and he said abruptly as he passed a letter over to her, 'It's from Viv. She, it would appear, is overjoyed at our marriage, although she's possibly the only one, did she but know it. It would seem,' he added with a cold smile, 'that she, as she puts it, thought we were made for each other from the moment she met you.'

'Rod. . . .' Bobbie fingered the letter with agitated fingers.

'No, Bobbie,' he cut in, 'the time for talking is long past.'

'But. . . .' She shrank from the sudden look of anger in his eyes.

He said as if she hadn't spoken, 'Something's come up, by the way. I'm negotiating for the lease of an

American stallion to stand at Horsham.' He added in clipped tones, 'Viv and I run a stud farm in partnership up there, in case you didn't know.'

'I . . . didn't,' she said quietly. 'I mean I did, but only because Ted Wilson told me once.'

'If you hadn't been so totally self-absorbed, Bobbie, I'm sure that would have entered your calculations too.'

Bobbie gasped at the unfairness of the attack and she knew with a painful bitter knowledge that in Rod's eyes she was not only a calculating, conniving person but a mercenary one at that.

He went on, disregarding her distraught look, 'The lessors of this stallion are in Sydney at the moment and I'm flying up to meet them tomorrow morning, and after that I'll be flying to Horsham to check up on a few things. Let's see . . . I should be back by Friday. Do you think you and Des can cope?'

'Yes,' she said quietly.

He stared at her thoughtfully for a few moments and then pushed his chair back and stood up. 'You can have the day off today,' he said casually, and turned towards the door.

Bobbie found her voice. 'No, thanks, Rod. There's no need. . . .'

But before she could finish he swung round on his heel and said tautly, 'Bobbie, from now on you do as I say, when I say it, or accept the consequences. Do you understand me, Bobbie?'

She said doggedly, 'I always do as you tell me. . . .' Her voice trailed off and she flushed as his sardonic gaze roamed from her now hot face down to rest at the open vee-neck of her flannel blouse.

'With one notable exception,' he said dryly. 'But we'll

be rectifying that. You have a charming body, my sweet little wife—at least that part of it you've allowed me to see so far. I must warn you, though, that I don't have unlimited patience and it wouldn't take a lot to make me tear every stitch of clothing off you and savour each and every part of you whether you were willing or not.' He opened the door, but stopped on the doorstep to add casually, 'So you'll take the day off, Bobbie, for two reasons. One, because I say so, and two, because we've been invited out to dinner tonight. It's a formal affair, so you can spend the time doing whatever it is women do for a change. I'd rather you didn't look like a hastily assembled ex-stable boy tonight.'

Bobbie stared at the closed door, but she wasn't seeing it. Instead, his words—'tearing every stitch of clothing off you'—kept repeating themselves through her brain until finally she closed her eyes and allowed her head to droop languidly like a bright flower, on one hand. Those words had conjured up a feeling of sensuality that even went beyond what she had felt the previous evening before Marianne's phone call, and she knew in her heart of hearts that if he ever did make good his threat, she wouldn't want to resist him. She shivered suddenly and stood up restlessly to collect the dirty dishes.

By the time she had tidied the house she had made a decision—a mad, rash one, she decided with a rueful grin, but it was as if someone or something outside of her was directing her. She wrote a note and left it on the table and after a quick spruce-up, got into her little yellow car and set out in the direction of Kilmore.

It was Vivian who had introduced her to the new

beauty salon in the town and they had both had their hair done there for her wedding. But today Bobbie decided that she would have the whole works, a hairdo, a facial and a manicure.

The whole process took hours, but Bobbie found herself revelling in it all, and when the time came for her hair to be styled she left the decision to the very competent hairdresser who said to her, 'You know, Mrs Simpson, I think your hair is long enough now to put up. Shall we try it?'

'If you think it would suit me. I want to look a bit special for tonight,' she confessed.

'I think it would. You have beautiful bone structure, and as for your eyes ... well ... but what I thought of doing was piling it on top of your head in a knot like this and just coaxing a few curls down to frame your face. What do you think?'

Bobbie stared at herself in the mirror. 'I like it,' she said finally. 'It makes me look—sophisticated, but will it stay up?'

The hairdresser laughed, 'Don't worry about that, I'll make it secure, but it will still look natural.'

And finally she was out of the salon with, but one last errand, which took her to the chemist.

She hesitated in front of the perfume cabinet for some time before a girl about her own age came to her rescue.

'Can I help you? It's rather bewildering choosing a perfume, isn't it?'

'Oh yes,' Bobbie said gratefully. 'I want a good French perfume, something special.'

'Is it for yourself?' the assistant enquired.

Bobbie nodded.

The girl looked at her and smiled suddenly. She said,

'I hope you don't think I'm crazy, but I know of one that's just perfect for you—this one here, Miss Dior. If I was ever trying to advertise it, I'd use you as the advertisement.'

Bobbie was taken aback, but she couldn't help feeling a warmth, although she knew her hairdo should take most of the credit for this unsought-after praise. And it was with an added feeling of confidence that she drove home.

Now all I've got to do is get myself to my room somehow without being seen, she told herself as she drove into the garage. Because I don't intend to be sighted until I'm dressed.

But Rod and Des were nowhere to be seen and she made herself some coffee and sandwiches, took them up to her room and shut the door firmly.

Several hours later when the sun had set, she heard Rod's footsteps in the passage, followed by a light knock on the door.

'Are you there, Bobbie?'

'Yes—I'm getting dressed,' she answered, and felt her heart thump.

'Right,' he said, 'we'll be leaving in half an hour.' And his footsteps receded towards the bathroom.

Bobbie took a deep breath and reached for her dress. This was the moment of truth, she thought, and then rephrased—when Rod saw her in it, that would be the moment of truth.

Tracey had talked her into buying it, but she had been dubious about it ever since. And as she slipped it on and reached behind her to do up the long zip she felt a tremor of apprehension as the dress settled around her.

She stared at herself critically in the long mirror, and

had to admit it was a beautiful dress. The grey chiffon that covered a taffeta underslip was covered in cob-webby swirls of glittering sequins and delicate diamanté patterns, and as she twirled gently the light caught them and the whole dress seemed to come alive with a silver fire. The design was very simple, a low-cut fitted bodice with very narrow shoulder straps, and a long skirt that hugged her slender hips, but as she twirled again the bottom of the skirt belled out gently.

She slid her feet, encased in the sheerest of nylons, into silver sandals of the finest kid and then bent to examine her make-up minutely. Again, as Vivian had shown her, she had used the barest minimum, although as well as darkening her lashes tonight she had used some silvery green eye-shadow.

She added an extra dash of lip-gloss and turned to check her silver evening bag again. And finally, as she heard Rod's footsteps going down stairs, she hesitated with the grey velvet jacket that came with the dress and had matching diamanté embroidery on the stand-up collar, in her hand. Should she put it on now or. . . .'

A little later, she thought—and closed her eyes suddenly in exasperation. Just what are you planning tonight, Bobbie . . . Simpson? she asked herself. I wish I knew, she answered her own question. I wish I knew. . . .

Rod was standing in the middle of the room as she hesitated at the top of the stairs. He paused in the act of raising a small glass of sherry to his lips as she descended slowly. But his eyes never left her until she was standing on the bottom step, suddenly unsure of herself and very tempted to run from the look in his eyes.

He put his glass down slowly and pushed his hands

into the pockets of his black dinner suit as he let his eyes roam over her, taking in the plunging neckline of her dress and her creamy shoulders with their faint golden bloom.

She stood quite still as if mesmerised, which indeed she was. Then Rod reached into an inner pocket of his jacket and moved towards her.

'You've done well, Bobbie,' he murmured. 'I think this will just complete the picture.'

It was a necklace he drew from his pocket, a delicate strand of silver supporting a diamond pendant. She gave a tiny gasp as she saw the diamond lying in his hand reflecting the firelight with a brilliant radiance, then she felt his strong hands about her neck as he clasped the jewel around her throat.

'There,' he said, and she felt a jolt of surprise at the husky note in his voice and the feel of his fingers as he set the stone in the valley of her small high breasts which the dress revealed.

She looked up from under her lashes, but his grey eyes were shrouded with a look of implacability that sent a tiny shiver down her spine and she faltered in the act of thanking him.

He said with a tinge of irony, 'Bobbie, this doesn't come free, gratis and for nothing, in case you think it did.'

'What . . . do you mean?' she stammered.

His eyes narrowed, but he said evenly enough, 'It means, my dearest wife, that having tried every other method to gain your favours, and failed signally, I'm now resorting to a tried and tested method. I suppose you could call it bartering. They say everyone has their price. Perhaps this bauble will be yours. Because if you intend to wear it tonight I intend to take it as tacit approval for the plans I have when we get home later, which include viewing this diamond in a slightly different setting—just adorning your naked body on its own.'

'Oh!' The exclamation was wrenched from her as a tide of hot colour suffused her face and neck. 'You . . . I . . . that's—horrible! You're. . . .'

But she didn't finish, because he turned with a cruel laugh at the sound of a hooter outside and drawled, 'It would appear that our companions have arrived. Did I tell you we were making up a foursome tonight?'

The evening passed in a curious blur for Bobbie. In the moments before Rod opened the door at the sound of the hooter, she had tried desperately to get the necklace off, but the tiny clasp had eluded her manicured but as yet modestly short fingernails. And then it had been too late. The couple they were joining, a fellow trotting driver and his wife whom Bobbie knew slightly, had accepted Rod's invitation to join them in a sherry before they set out together, and Bobbie found herself the recipient of their compliments not only for her dress and appearance, but her jewellery as well.

The dinner party was at the Golf Club once more, but this time a private one, and was being held, Bobbie discovered, to honour a retiring driver who had achieved the feat of driving over five hundred metropolitan winners during his long career. And once again she discovered she was the centre of some attraction. But if she got through the evening with a certain mechanical quality, no one seemed to notice and no one commented.

No one at least, except Rod himself, and his mocking

comment, delivered during the one dance she had with him, didn't exactly ease the situation.

He said, 'Bobbie, it might be an idea if you tried to look as if you were enjoying this.'

'Well, I'm not,' she said baldly. 'I very much resent your insinuations that I can be bought!'

'But I see you're still wearing the necklace,' he said with one eyebrow raised cynically.

'That's only because I couldn't get it off!' she retorted hotly, and added, 'I mean, without making a silly scene.'

She gasped as his arms tightened cruelly around her, but she kept her eyes on him bravely as he said tightly. 'You're in a fair way to making a scene here, though. But it isn't on. We'll continue this—discussion later.' And as the music faded he led her back to their table with an iron hand around her arm.

But finally, the almost nightmare evening was over and they were back home again on their own, although a glance at his grim face as he threw a log on the fire made Bobbie wonder if perhaps the nightmare was only just beginning.

She stood irresolutely in the middle of the room until he straightened finally. He stood with his back to the now flaming fire and with his hands pushed deep into his pockets surveyed her broodingly.

From sheer fright she found herself saying, 'Would . . . you like a cup of coffee?'

'Thank you,' he said coolly.

The small chore was soon accomplished and Bobbie carried the two steaming cups over to the fireplace. He took his and set it on the mantelpiece. She hovered uncertainly for a moment, wondering what his reaction would be if she said she would like to take hers up to her room. She didn't have long to wonder.

He said, 'Sit down, Bobbie.'

She hestiated and then sank down into an armchair. She found her heart was pounding uncomfortably and she couldn't for the life of her imagine how she was going to handle the coming situation. But as she looked down, the glint of the diamond caught her eye and she felt again the searing contempt of what he had said earlier. She put her cup down beside her and noted with inward surprise that her fingers didn't tremble at all as she pulled the clasp of the necklace around to the front and undid it.

She felt his gaze searing her as the brilliant stone lay in her hand for a moment. Then she put it down on the coffee table and picked up her cup. The silence lengthened and the only two sounds to mar it were the crackle of the flames in the grate and the uneasy thump of Bluey's tail on the rug.

Bobbie looked around the room. It was warm and cosy in the firelight with only one small table lamp adding to the glow, but she shivered suddenly and forced herself to look at Rod at last. He was staring down at the necklace and then his lashes lifted and she shivered again and thought that she'd never seen his eyes so cold.

But when he spoke his voice was even enough, although with that familiar mocking tinge. He said, 'I gather you're trying to tell me you can't be bought, Bobbie?'

'I . . . yes.'

He moved suddenly and threw himself down into the

armchair opposite. 'Perhaps then, if that's the case, you'd care to explain to me just why you did marry me, Bobbie? I confess I'm at a loss.'

She knitted her fingers together and tried desperately to work out what she could say to him. She started to speak several times, but halted each time in hopeless confusion.

Finally Rod said softly but with a faint note of menace in his voice, 'Come here, Bobbie.'

She jumped. 'I. . . . No!'

'Yes. Or shall I come and get you?'

She scrambled up. 'No, Rod, please!'

But with one lithe movement he was on his feet and his hands shot out to imprison hers as she took a step backwards and tripped on the edge of the rug. She tried to fight him, but it was useless, and he swung her up into his arms and carried her upstairs and into his bedroom, where he flung her on to the bed and turned coolly to close the door.'

She got to her knees cautiously while his back was turned and moved to the other side of the bed awkwardly, hampered by her long skirt and conscious that her hair-do wasn't proof against this kind of treatment and was now tumbling around her shoulders. But he turned as she slid off the other side of the bed and with a mocking glance rested his broad shoulders against the closed door.

'I wouldn't try the window if I were you. You'd break your neck.'

She stared at him furiously and said through clenched teeth, 'Let me out of here this instant, Rod, or I'll . . . or I'll. . . .'

'Or you'll what?' he drawled, his mouth quirking with

amusement. 'Scream? Fall down in a maidenly swoon?' He pushed himself away from the door and with a negligent movement removed his tie and jacket. 'So? What's it to be, Bobbie? Because I'm not letting you out of here just yet.' And he moved towards her with the lazy grace of a panther intent on its prey.

But the spreading numbness she had begun to feel was suddenly dissipated and she flew at him, as furiously angry as she had ever been in her life and intent on striking him with all her might.

'I—hate you!' she panted, and then, 'Let me go!' as her puny resistance was smothered in his hard embrace. 'Please. . . .'

'Not yet, my little wildcat,' he said roughly, and lifted her bodily on to the bed once more. 'Don't fight me any more, Bobbie, you'll only get hurt.'

She tried to twist away, but he released his grasp on her wrists and sat down beside her, effectively imprisoning her with an arm planted on the bed on either side of her. He murmured, 'You look very beautiful when you're angry, my sweet.' His grey eyes roamed from her face to her heaving breasts. 'And that dress is quite sensational. A fitting frame for you, but the time has come now to remove the frame. . . .'

One hand came up and he touched a lock of her fiery hair, and he grinned suddenly. 'I wonder if any of our kids will have red hair—and a temper to match!'

Bobbie lay like a frozen statue and his smile faded slowly, but his hand moved down her neck to rest briefly on her shoulder. Still she didn't—couldn't—stir, and with an impatient sound Rod slipped his fingers beneath her and released the zipper of her dress.

A tremor passed down the length of her spine at the

feel of his fingers on her bare flesh. She brought both arms up in a gesture of resistance as his hands slipped beneath the straps of her dress and pushed them off her shoulders, but the small resistance died at the grim, intent look on his face.

He undressed her slowly and carefully but with an economic precision, until her breath was coming in ragged gasps and she was unable to control the fine trembling of her body. His hands lingered on her thighs as he drew the sheer fine tights from her legs, and she knew without doubt that she had fallen victim to the strange, compelling delight that each of his gestures caused to pervade her.

She lay with her eyes closed, conscious of nothing but his strong hands on her, then there was a small respite and she wanted to cry out to him not to stop, but she was afraid to open her eyes in case she should see amusement or mockery in his.

She lay rigid with her arms pressed to her sides, caught in a web of shyness that seemed to enmesh her with bars of steel. Then she felt the bed sag beneath his weight as he lay beside her and took her in his arms, and she revelled exultantly but silently at the feel of his strong hard body against her own.

I have only to bring my hands up to—touch him, to caress his shoulders, she told herself, and then he'll know that I'm not hating this. Far from it. . . .'

But even as the thought transmitted itself to action, the sound of a klaxon split the deep, quiet night and a powerful engine revved mightily to be cut almost immediately.

Bobbie froze, an instinctive reaction from sheer surprise, and heard Rod swear forcefully.

'What . . . what is it?' she whispered as he left the bed. Her eyes flew open, but she shut them again at the sight of his lean, lithe body with its powerful shoulders and slim hips.

'It's the horse transport,' he said in clipped tones. 'I've bought a new horse from Adelaide, and this must be it arriving now. These transport chaps make a habit of arriving in the middle of the night. Their schedules don't make allowances for other people's sleep patterns—or other activities,' he added sardonically.

A small desolate sigh escaped her.

'You can open your eyes now, Bobbie. I'm dressed,' she heard him drawl.

Her lids fluttered open reluctantly to see him standing over her. His expression was controlled, but she noticed a nerve throbbing in his jaw as he said, 'It would appear you've been saved from a fate worse than death—once again, my dear.'

She flinched at the contempt in his voice.

'Rod, I. . . .' she whispered desperately.

But he went on as if she hadn't spoken, 'There'll be other nights, though, Bobbie, and there'll be no phone calls, no horse transports to intrude. In fact there will be only one difference.'

She stared at him wide-eyed and he allowed his steely grey gaze to roam over her from head to toe, bringing a tide of rosy colour to her cheeks, before he said quietly, 'One difference. You do realise I could have done this any time since we were married, Bobbie, don't you? But I held back out of—possibly misguided—consideration for you. Things have changed now, though. You married me for better or worse, and if you continue to make heavy weather of it, that's your lookout. Because from now on this will be a proper marriage. In every respect,' he added almost casually as he turned away and went out of the room.

CHAPTER ELEVEN

Bobbie woke with a start and looked around anxiously, for a moment unsure of where she was. But the dim light of early morning revealed her own familiar room and she lay back with a sigh.

Of course, she remembered now. She had waited for Rod on his bed with the coverlet clutched around her. Waited until she heard the horse transport depart noisily. Waited as she heard the opening and closing of the outside door and the sounds of him moving around downstairs. But he hadn't come up and finally, feeling more desolate and unhappy then she could ever recall, she had gathered up her clothes and with his coverlet still clutched around her, she had crept stealthily down the passage to her room.

Sleep had come a long time later, and as she looked at her bedside clock, she realised that she had overslept. And yet she found it hard to persuade herself to get up, and her mind kept returning to those earlier hours and she relived again those magical moments when she had lain on Rod's bed with his hands on her.

Why, oh, why didn't I respond, she asked herself the same question over and over, until it was too late? Why . . .?

The roar of a motor disturbed these torturous thoughts and she sat up with a jerk. It was Rod's car. Of course! He was flying up to Sydney today. And he was going without saying goodbye. Bobbie leapt out of

bed and ran to the window just in time to see the low
grey sports car nose out of the driveway and with a
powerful surge of acceleration disappear down the
road.

There was a note for her on the table, she found
when she got downstairs. It was brief and terse.

'Don't contemplate running away, Bobbie, because if
it's the last thing I do, I'll find you. Rod.'

She knew it was cowardly to admit to a certain feeling of relief some time later in the morning at the lack
of Rod's presence, but at least, as she told Bluey, it gave
her some time to marshal her defences and sort out her
emotions. But by the end of the day she was no further
forward with her problems, and as she did the evening chores on her own, because it was Des's half
day off, she found she was moving round in a semi-
dazed fashion—a combination of numbness and quiet
despair. Which was possibly how she came to overlook
something she would not have in any other circumstances.

And it was only later as she was eating her own solitary meal that this something that had been nagging her
subconscious crystallised in her mind, and with a
sudden exclamation she dropped her knife and fork and
dashed out into the dark, freezing night without even
stopping to don her coat.

She found she was praying silently as she ran down
to the stables and struggled with the stiff lock on the
shed door. It yielded finally and she switched on the
light and ran along the row of stalls until she came to
Morningtown's box, and the sight that greeted her eyes
confirmed her worst fears. There was no doubt that the
horse was now distressed, and Bobbie cursed herself for

not taking notice of the earlier signs, for being too wrapped up in her own to problems for it to penetrate that for the first time since she had known the horse, he had scorned his feed bin.

She watched him critically for a moment as he stood there in an uncharacteristically dejected pose with his head hanging low and his flanks heaving, then he turned his head to bunt it impatiently at one flank, and she sprang into action.

She had seen colic before and she knew just how quickly it could develop into a twisted bowel condition which was fatal for a horse. She grabbed his headstall and snapped it on together with a strong lead, and by dint of much patient urging and tugging she persuaded the distraught horse to leave his box, then led to him to a harnessing bay and tied him up securely in cross leads and flew immediately to the stable extension. But after five minutes of frantic dialling and finally some desperate banging on the wickedly inanimate telephone she realised it was not working, for some reason.

She cast the now very restless horse an agonised glance and decided immediately that she had to risk leaving him while she raced up to the house again to try the phone up there.

But that phone remained obstinately dead too, and she realised with a sense of panic that she was cut off from the rest of the world. She thought wildly of jumping into her car and going to fetch Des, but then she recalled that this was the first Tuesday of the month and it was Bingo night at the local church, which was a good twelve miles away and the entire Mead family never ever missed a Bingo night. Which held true for nearly all of her close neighbours.

'Oh, Bluey!' she sighed desperately. 'What shall I do? If I do a tour of the neighbourhood I still might not find anyone home and Morningtown could ... die while I'm gone!'

It was that awful thought that pulled her up short.

'No, Bluey,' she said, suddenly calm. 'Morningtown is not going to die while I'm here.'

She never afterwards knew how she did it, because she had never drenched a horse before, although she had seen it done. But somehow or other she managed to get the long narrow tube up his nostril and with a whispered prayer, one of the many she prayed in that long night, she poured the warm liquid paraffin she had prepared down it, hoping against desperate hope that she had the tube positioned correctly and wasn't pouring the stuff into his lungs.

And finally the lack of adverse reaction assured her that she had not, and she felt the taut muscles of her chest relax slightly and she thought, well, if I can do that I can do the other. She prepared an injection of a painkilling substance that she had seen her father and Rod use and without allowing herself to hesitate gave it to Morningtown with the assurance of a vet.

She stood back with the spent hypodermic in her hand and waited with her heart in her mouth. But the horse showed no tendency to keel over on her and she let out a relieved sigh.

She glanced down the aisle between the two rows of boxes. 'I've got to keep you on your feet now, old feller,' she told the distressed horse, 'but somehow I think we'll only create a furore if we parade up and down here between the boxes. As it is, they're all stirred up, so what we'll do is I'll rug you up snugly and we'll take a turn round the track.'

She put two thick rugs on him and cast around for something to wear herself, but all she could find was an old lightweight waterproof jacket of Rod's. It will just have to do, she told herself, because if I leave him now and he gets down to roll, I might as well not have bothered with the drench.

Looking back on the experience afterwards, she couldn't say what it was that kept her going through that long, cold night. Possibly a combination of the thought of Rod and her genuine, heart-stirring affection for his champion horse. But at the time all she knew was that she could not let Morningtown die before her eyes. Not Morningtown. . . .

So she walked him patiently, even though the jacket she wore wasn't proof against the biting cold, with one thought always in her mind. She couldn't afford to leave the horse in case he tried to go down. Because she knew that was when he could incur a twisted bowel as he rolled in agony.

And as she grew colder doubts rose up in her mind at the treatment she had given the horse.

I assumed it was colic, she told herself, but I'm not a vet. If it isn't colic I might have done all the wrong things . . . oh, God, please help me!

But what seemed like hours later, her diagnosis was proved correct, and feeling weak and lightheaded with relief, she put him back in his box and watched with joyous eyes as he moved around freely, then with a relaxed snort dropped his head to the feed bin which held a small feed and bran-mash she had fixed for him.

'But all the same, I'm not letting you out of my sight

tonight old son,' she told him warmly, and she gathered a pile of rugs and set them in front of his stall door and sat down to her vigil.

Bluey snuggled up to her and she pulled one of the rugs around them both. But try as she might she couldn't get warm, and she shivered miserably until a strange lethargy overtook her and she dropped off into an uneasy sleep.

'Bobbie!'

She jerked awake to stare unbelievingly at the tall figure standing before her.

'What the hell are you doing?' he ground out.

'I . . . I. . . .' she stammered, and found that her lips were dry and although she felt cold she seemed to be burning up at the same time and her chest felt curiously tight once more. 'You're in Sydney,' she said stupidly.

'I was in Sydney,' he corrected her tautly, 'until I tried to get hold of you on the phone. But you haven't answered my question. Why the bloody hell are you down here? And what have you done to the phones?'

'Nothing,' she whispered painfully. 'They just don't work. And Morningtown had colic, but . . . but he's all right now. See . . .?'

Rod's gaze sharpened suddenly and he knelt down beside her with an impatient exclamation and she heard him say roughly, 'Are you right, Bobbie? Bobbie!'

She moistened her lips with the tip of her tongue. 'I don't . . . I feel a little peculiar,' she faltered.

He took her shoulders in his hands and his eyes blazed at her, 'You little idiot! You've hardly got any clothes on and it's freezing. Don't you know anything? It seems I can't let you out of my sight for a minute!' And he shook her.

'Don't,' she whispered pleadingly, 'my head. . . .'

'Bobbie. . . .' she heard him say in exasperation. 'God help me, but you drive me to distraction!' And he swung her up into his arms.

'I'm so sorry to be such a nuisance. . . .'

'Don't be,' he said on a gentler note, 'the main thing is to get you warm now.'

'I feel very warm,' she murmured, and then shivered violently.

Rod tightened his arms around her, but she didn't hear what he muttered under his breath as he carried her up to the house.

A car drove in as he reached the doorstep and Des stepped out.

'Rod!' he exclaimed in surprise. 'What are you doing here?'

'Don't worry about what I'm doing here,' Rod said curtly, 'but perhaps you can tell me what's going on around here. And why you're driving around at two o'clock in the morning.' He put Bobbie gently down in an armchair and with a curse knelt before the fire that was now dead. 'But first of all help me get this damn fire going, will you?'

Bobbie was dimly able to comprehend the whole story which Des related while Rod wrapped her in blankets and then forced some spiked coffee between her chattering lips.

Someone had collided with a telephone pole about five miles away and brought down a whole section of line. And unfortunately the combination of the fact that the driver of the car was knocked unconscious in the collision, together with the fact that most of the phones affected belonged, as Bobbie had foreseen, to people who had gone out to the Bingo night, had delayed discovery of the incident. Des himself had gone to a friend's house for a midnight supper after the Bingo, and it was while he was there that he learnt of it.

He said, 'Straight away I started to wonder about Bobbie and the horses just in case anything went wrong. That's why I'm here now.'

'Good on you, mate,' Rod said briefly. 'According to Bobbie, Morningtown chose this of all nights to get colic. She's been with him for hours, by the look of it. Any idea when the line will be fixed?'

Des shook his head. 'Could be some time, Rod. They have to get a crew out, and it's only a country line, you know.'

'Right,' Rod said abruptly. 'How far away is the nearest doctor?'

'Doc Benson? About ten miles, I guess.'

'Okay, you hop in your car, Des, and go and get him and bring him back with you even if you have to drag him out of bed. Tell him it might be pneumonia and I don't want to drag the patient out into the cold again.'

'Will do, Rod.' Des cast Bobbie an anxious look and walked out swiftly.

Bobbie opened her eyes to see Rod standing over her. She tried to smile, but shivered again instead.

'Bobbie,' he said gently, 'I've got to get you warm. I'm going to bring a mattress down here and put it in front of the fire. O.K.?'

She nodded.

And several minutes later he had made a bed for her in front of the fire and lifted her on to it. He stood looking down at her for a moment as she tried desperately to control the shivers that racked her body, then he closed his eyes briefly and with a swift movement lay down beside her and took her into his arms.

'Perhaps this will work,' he murmured into her hair as he held her close. 'Just try and relax, Bobbie.'

And finally, with her head cradled on his shoulder and his arms still around her holding her pressed to the warm, strong length of him, she stopped shivering and fell into a light sleep.

She stirred restlessly as he moved at the sound of a car outside and murmured drowsily, 'Don't . . . go away.'

'I'll be back,' he said, and dropped a light kiss on her hair.

What was left of the night passed in a blur for Bobbie, as did the next day, for that matter, and it was the following morning before she found she was lucid and able to stay awake for any length of time. And the first conversation she had was with Doctor Benson.

'Well, Bobbie,' he said as he put his bag down on her bedside table, 'It's good to see you looking brighter. I must say you gave us all a bit of a fright, and I came very close to sending you to hospital, young lady.'

Bobbie smiled weakly. 'I feel better,' she said.

'You can thank your husband and Mrs Mead for that, Bobbie, because without his prompt action and her careful nursing it would have been a lot worse.' He shook his head and smiled at her before he said, 'Tell me, Bobbie, what had you being doing to yourself before you got this raging chill? Because you know, young lady, I couldn't help noticing that you're a bit on the skinny side and you didn't seem to have quite as much resistance as I would have expected from a healthy young thing.'

'Nothing,' she said with a look of surprise.

'At least—well, I suppose I haven't been eating too well lately, but. . . .'

'I thought as much,' he said severely, 'I'll never understand young ladies! Anyhow, I'm going to recommend to Rod that as soon as you feel well enough to travel, he takes you away for a good holiday.'

'Oh no, Doctor Benson!' She sat up urgently.

A voice spoke from the doorway. 'Oh yes, Bobbie. If that's the doctor's advice.'

Rod strolled into the room and stood with his arms folded across his chest and the light of battle in his grey eyes.

The doctor spoke soothingly. 'It's for the best, my dear.' He stood up and gathered together his things. 'And now I'll leave you two to discuss things, but I'll be back tomorrow, Rod, for a final check-up.'

Bobbie was staring miserably at the wall when Rod came back into the room, having seen the doctor on his way. He sat down on the bed and took one of her hands in his. 'Do you feel well enough to talk, Bobbie?'

'Yes.'

'It might help if you looked at me,' he said with a trace of amusement in his voice.

Oh no, it won't, she thought rebelliously. Because all I'll think about is lying in his arms, which is about the only thing I remember quite clearly. But the power of his personality was too strong for her and she turned to him reluctantly.

He said quietly, 'I owe you a great debt of gratitude. I don't know how you managed it single-handed, but I'll never forget what you did for Morningtown.'

'How . . . how is he?' she asked with a catch in her voice.

'A lot better than you are, Bobbie,' he said wryly.

'And thanks to you I can't see any reason not to start him in ten days' time as I'd planned. There's a cup race coming up for him at Moonee Valley on Saturday week.'

She sighed. 'I'm so pleased.'

Rod waited for a moment, then he said, 'Bobbie, I think the doctor's right. You need a break, perhaps—from me as well as everything else. Much as I'd like to, I can't get away for any length of time now, so I thought it would be an idea for you to go and stay with Tracey for a week or so. Steve's in New Guinea at the moment and I know she'd welcome some company. With the doctor's permission I'll drive you down tomorrow.'

'I. . . .' Bobbie stopped. She had been going to say that she could convalesce just as well at Greentree Farm as anywhere else and that she wouldn't be any trouble to him, but then she thought Rod must know this. And yet for some reason he wasn't suggesting it.

'Very well,' she said.

'Good girl!' He pressed her hand and stood up, and she realised then that those tiny hopes that she had been unconsciously nurturing, that the time spent in his arms in front of the fire had been special, were not, but only what he would have done for anyone, no more, no less. And the realisation came as a shocking blow.

CHAPTER TWELVE

TRACEY's home was warm and comfortable and in any other circumstances Bobbie would have enjoyed her stay and enjoyed for once being fussed over. And indeed, despite herself, she did enjoy the first few days, and particularly Tracey's company, but as the time passed and Rod stayed away, although he rang most days, she grew quieter and paler.

Tracey didn't press her, but Bobbie knew she was waiting for her to say something. She did contemplate baring her heart to Tracey and several times actually came close to doing it, but something held her back each time. After all, as she told herself, Tracey would only reiterate her earlier advice and Bobbie had already found that this was what she could not do.

The slow days trickled by until nearly ten days had passed since she had seen Rod. And each day had been a special form of torture for her, waiting for the sound of his car in the driveway, his footfall on the doorstep.

It was on a Friday that she finally came to a decision, a decision prompted by two factors—the increasing look of desperation in Tracey's eyes and a picture in the morning paper attached to the trot fields for the following day.

As Rod had promised, Morningtown was having his first start in his current preparation in Melbourne, the next day, and as was common practice when dealing with a horse of his calibre, the press was devoting some attention to him. Not only was there a picture of him in the paper but an article detailing the highlights of his illustrious career. Bobbie had trouble checking the tears as she read the article. Because although she had spoken to Rod the previous day, he had made no mention of Morningtown and no suggestion that she should be at Moonee Valley to watch him run. But as upsetting as this was, the picture accompanying the article was more so, because even though it was slightly blurred as newpaper pictures are sometimes, Bobbie had no difficulty in identifying not only the horse but the girl standing proudly at his head while Rod sat in the gig. It was Marianne Hunter.

And that just about sums it all up, Bobbie, she told herself. I was a fool to ever think I could compete, and there only remains one thing to be done. Just to disappear quietly and efficiently.

But even this decision posed some problems. Should she tell Tracey or not?

She argued this out with herself all morning and finally decided that to tell her would be placing an unfair burden on her. Better just to leave without Tracey knowing if she could manage it. I'll write a note absolving her of all responsibility, she thought—the only thing is, how to get out without arousing her suspicions?

But finally it was Tracey herself who solved this problem, for early in the afternoon she suddenly remembered she had a dentist's appointment.

'Bobbie, do you want to come into town with me? If I cancel this one it might be a month before I get another one.'

Bobbie pretended to consider for a minute before she

said, 'I don't think so, thanks, Tracey.' She held out the book she had been trying to read and added, at the same time feeling awful for the lies she was telling, 'I'm really getting into this book. I might just curl up in front of the fire with it. Besides, if Rod comes. . . .'

Tracey gace her a long look. 'If you're sure, Bobbie? I won't be very long. . . .'

'I'm sure, Tracey. Don't worry about me, I'll be fine.'

Bobbie looked around as she closed her suitcase, but she had left nothing and she walked slowly into the lounge room. She had written a note which said simply that Tracey was not to worry about her and to assure her of Bobbie's everlasting gratitude and affection.

She frowned with the note in her hand and then quickly pulled a pen from her pocket and added, 'I hope you can forgive me for doing this, Tracey, but I know it's the only way. Love, Bobbie.'

She placed the note on the mantelpiece and started at the sound of a hooter outside. But it was the taxi she had ordered and with a lingering backward glance, she made her way slowly out to it, unable to suppress the feeling of distaste she was experiencing for the way she was leaving.

The motel she chose was clean and respectable-looking, but a far cry from the luxury of the hotel Rod had taken her to, and this depressed her even more to the point of sinking down on the bed and indulging in a good cry. But somehow the tears seemed to have a steadying effect and when she finally blew her nose it was with a feeling of resolution and even some relief. However painful the decision had been and would always be, at least it had been made.

But the following evening, after a day spent trying to work out some kind of a future for herself and also wondering just how she would be able to get her car from Greentree Farm without revealing her whereabouts to Rod, she switched on the radio to get some light music, but instead her fingers stilled on the knob as she heard the familiar voice of the trot previewer.

'....would be well advised to brave the cold, for tonight at Moonee Valley we have a rare treat in store, in the form of Morningtown. I think I ran out of superlatives last year when he contested and won the A.G. Hunter Cup here in such great style, but the incredible news is that his owner-trainer, Rod Simpson, has moved his establishment to Victoria, so we will now have the opportunity to see much more of this great horse. I was only talking to Rod at Bendigo this week and he assured me that Morningtown is going as well as ever. ....'

No, Bobbie said to herself. No. It would be utter madness.

But another voice inside of her took over. You've never seen him race. Would it hurt to see him just this once? You could never be noticed in the crowd. ...

She was still arguing with herself as she paid off the taxi and made her way into the racecourse, until finally she told herself firmly that she was here now and she better make the best of it. All you've got to do is stay away from the horse area and you'll be all right, Bobbie!

And she held to this resolution for the first half of the night. She chose a seat in a remote corner of the furthest stand and after buying herself something to eat, she stayed put.

A quick glance through the race-book showed her that Rod had three drives that night, two early ones and then Morningtown, and it was with a sensation of breathlessness, almost, that she watched him steer the chestnut that had beaten Best Dressed at Kilmore what seemed like an eternity ago now, out on to the track for the second race.

Despite the colourful silks and white helmet he wore, every line of his lithe, powerful figure was dearly familiar to her, and she found she couldn't tear her eyes from him.

The chestnut horse ran a close second after galloping away again, and Bobbie knew how frustrated Rod must be feeling because he had put a lot of work into trying to get the horse to step cleanly. There was no doubt that the horse had plenty of potential, if only it could be persuaded to square up to a tape.

The next race didn't hold much interest for her and she took the opportunity to study the crowd. It would seem that Morningtown had attracted a lot of people despite the cold weather, and for a little while Bobbie felt a surge of quiet contentment as the colourful crowd surged and ebbed. She listened to the familiar talk that she had been hearing all her life, and saw before her the track gleaming whitely under the powerful lights, edged by the green of the galloping track and beyond, into the clear, cold night, the lights of Melbourne.

Then Rod was back on the track, this time driving a powerful-looking black horse that she didn't recognise. She consulted the book and discovered that this horse belonged to someone else for whom Rod must have consented to drive.

But it was obvious, as soon as it set foot on the track

proper, that this horse was going to be a handful, and she knew as if she could read his mind that Rod would be cursing it grimly.

She watched with her heart in her mouth as the horse played up at the start, rearing and prancing, and although she knew that if anyone was equal to the task of controlling it, Rod was, she still could not suppress a taste of fear for him and she understood just what Tracey must have gone through.

But finally the starter got the field away and the black horse bounded to the lead, and she clicked her tongue in annoyance because it was soon obvious that the horse had but one thought in its brain—and that was to bolt with Rod. She watched him lying back in the gig with his arms stretched out, and felt the sweat break out on her brow.

Then, almost imperceptibly, the pressure eased and he was sitting upright in the gig with the horse now accepting his dictates, and the man beside her was saying, '. . . . he's close to being a genius, Simpson is. I've see with my own eyes that mongrel horse climb the fence with some poor idiot in the gig, but look at him now, he's going round like a little lamb! I tell you. . . .'

But the early effort told on the horse and it could only manage to finish fourth, then her neighbour was talking loudly again, '. . . . should give him a medal. It's the first time the horse has finished in a place. . . .'

She sat back and tried to relax, for Morningtown's was the next race on the card. The half-hour between races passed slowly, but a sudden stir in the crowd told her that Morningtown had finally appeared.

Bobbie watched the two of them with tears in her eyes as Morningtown paced around in his preliminary.

He looked magnificent, she thought, and the comments around her told her that the crowd agreed with this. She saw with surprise that there was not a seat to spare anywhere around her, and yet as the horses lined up for the start, the crowd was quiet and she could feel a tension in the air and realised that this was the sensation this horse would produce wherever he went.

At least I was associated with him for a little while, she told herself. Better, surely, than never to have known him. . . .

Then the tapes flew back and Morningtown paced away perfectly from his backline handicap and tacked on to the main body of the field with little effort. The race was a copybook one until the last lap, then challenges came thick and fast and the lead changed hands several times, but still Morningtown sat at the tail of the field, with Rod relaxed and unmoving in the gig.

Bobbie held her breath as the field flew out of the last bend and into the home straight, and the crowd rose to its feet with a collective roar as Rod made his move to take the horse wide of the field. Morningtown grabbed the bit and set sail for home gaining on them stride by stride, with a devastatingly powerful sprint that took him to the winning post to win by lengths.

The course announcer's voice had been totally drowned in the tumult of the last stages of the race, and now by the rousing cheer and standing reception the crowd gave Rod and Morningtown, and Bobbie found she was on her feet cheering as hard as anyone as Rod came back to scale and doffed his helmet to the crowd.

But the noise had diminished somewhat by the time the all-clear was sounded, and Bobbie sank back into her seat to hear the announcer say, 'We now have the offical time and totes. The race was won by Number Ten, Morningtown, a six-year-old brown stallion by Townfair out of Morning Light, owned by Mr and Mrs R. Simpson and trained and driven by R. Simpson. . . .'

It took a moment for this to sink in and then Bobbie heard herself saying out loud, 'That can't be right! Morningtown's raced by Moreton Holdings—I know because I saw it on his assessment card. . . .'

Her eyes flew to the race book that was still open in her hands and for a second the black type danced before her eyes. But it was down in the book too. Mr & Mrs R. Simpson's Morningtown. . . .

What does it mean? she asked herself agitatedly. It must be a mistake, because Viv and Rod own Morningtown and they race it in their company's name. How come . . .?

She sat there with flushed cheeks and a pounding heart. What if it wasn't a mistake? she asked herself. Oh, but it had to be! She stood up restlessly and made her way downstairs, and as if drawn by some powerful magnet, found herself drifting towards the horse stalls.

She didn't recognise anybody in the the eager throng of people surging around the betting ring, but all the same she took care to mingle with the crowd as she passed under an archway and came out at the marshalling yard.

Not that I'm so recognisable, she thought suddenly with a tiny grin, because for some reason she had taken great care in choosing her clothes and she was wearing a woollen suit in a soft green that had a matching green silk blouse to go with it and tan leather accessories. Tracey had helped her to choose the outfit and even at the time she had found difficulty in recognising the elegant creature who had stared back at her from the mirror when she had tried it on.

But all the same, when she discovered that most of the crowd seemed to be headed for Morningtown's stall, she hesitated and hung back for a moment before allowing herself to drift along with them.

But she need not have worried, because there was already a crowd gathered to stare at their idol, and she realised that from the other side of the fence it would be very difficult to pick one individual out of it. And she took her time to stare her fill at the horse and his driver.

Morningtown looked fresh enough almost to run another race as Des dried him down, but Bobbie couldn't quite say the same for Rod. He had his helmet off and he was leaning back against the stall wall with his arms folded across his chest, and for a minute she was stunned to see how weary he looked as he talked desultorily with an official who had a pleased grin on his face.

She studied his face, noting the new lines etched on it, and her heart faltered as he raised a hand and pulled it through his hair in a familiar gesture that was somehow new because it lacked his usual self-assurance, then he straightened up and squared his shoulders as if they were stiff, which she knew suddenly they would be after driving that black horse, and she felt an incredible longing to be able to massage the pain and the stiffness away. But he turned towards the fence and she took fright immediately and melted into the crowd.

Back once more in her plain, cheerless motel room, she got ready for bed with her emotions again in a dreadful turmoil.

What if Rod had made an incredible gesture and given her a half-share in Morningtown? Perhaps he had done it out of gratitude for her saving the horse when he had colic? Could it be that? she asked herself, and answered her own question for the tenth time at least. That could be the only explanation—provided the whole thing wasn't a mistake. And how had she repaid that gesture? By running away like a coward.

Oh, what a fool you are, Bobbie, she told herself. Even if he couldn't give you his love, a gift like this comes pretty close, because I doubt if even Marianne means more to him than Morningtown.

During the long night, she tossed and turned, and when she did drift off to sleep it was to find herself dreaming of horses and races and herself driving Morningtown and being beaten on him, and Rod's angry face.

It was as she was watching the sunrise that she thought of her father, and one of his maxims came to mind. He had always said to her, 'Bobbie, you'll find out for yourself that there's only one way to be in this life, however hard it seems, and that's truthful and open.'

But right from the start, she reminded herself, I was never open with Rod. I was always too worried about making a fool of myself, always thinking of me and my feelings. Surely if I don't owe him anything else, at least I owe him an honest explanation now. It's the least I can do, and I can clear the way for him and Marianne to get together. Because even if he didn't mention her by name, he did level with me, and he did make this gesture.

The car she had hired purred along the country roads, and she sighed with relief as she left the city behind her and drove the seventy-odd miles to Greentree Farm.

The day was cold but clear and bright with no wind, and the sky overhead was deep blue and cloudless. And all around her, the paddocks wore their winter colour of pale gold. It was a perfect winter's day and she took pleasure in it, but nevertheless as she got closer to the farm, she found her hands starting to shake.

What if he's furious with me? she asked herself, and sighed deeply.

Nothing had changed about the farm as she drove up the drive. The house sat sleepily in the midday sun and horses browsed contentedly in the paddocks that swept up to hilltop and the great tree that stood there.

Bobbie stepped out of the car and was immediately besieged by Bluey, who lolled his tongue foolishly at her and wriggled his body in an ectasy of affection. She bent to pat him and return his greeting, and when she straightened up it was to see that Rod had come up the stable pathway and was standing silently watching them both with an expresionless face.

She started and felt the old, treacherous colour flood her cheeks.

'I . . . I came,' she stammered, 'to talk to you.'

His eyes searched her face and he said finally, 'Come inside.'

Bobbie followed him in and sent up swift prayer—Oh God, please help me.

She stopped on the doorstep and looked around the large room in surprise. For it bore evidence of some neglect, and she flicked him a startled glance. But if he noticed her surprise he didn't comment, and it was only when she was seated at the oak table with a cup of coffee before her that he spoke.

'What did you think of Morningtown last night, Bobbie?' he asked abruptly.

'I . . . how did you know?' she whispered.

He shrugged. 'I saw you.'

'I thought he was magnificent,' she said after a minute. 'Rod. . . .' And there she halted and coloured again.

'What is it, Bobbie?' he asked quietly.

She plaited her fingers. 'Rod, will you just let me say this without interupting and . . . and without getting angry?'

His gaze sharpened, but he merely nodded.

She said urgently, 'I'm *sorry* for the way I've behaved, particularly these last few days. It was . . . it was stupid to run away from Tracey and I regret it bitterly. And everything else I've done since I've known you. But you see I—well, I know the truth. I know that you love Marianne and always will. No, please,' she held up a hand, 'it doesn't matter how I know it. It makes no difference really.' She looked down at her hands and continued unsteadily, 'At first, I thought . . . I thought we could make a go of it, but then I discovered that you were *right*. I'm just not mature enough, perhaps, for that kind of an arrangement, and if I seemed unpredictable and unreasonable as I'm sure now, looking back, I must have, that's the reason. And I'm sorry,' she said again.

He didn't stir, but his eyes never left her face.

She went on gruffly, 'I rang up the Trotting Board this morning because I wasn't sure whether . . . whether it had been a mistake in the book last night about

. . . about our name as owners of Morningtown. They told me it was no mistake. I . . . I just want to say that I'll always be grateful, but I can't accept it.'

'Why not?'

She shot him a look from under her lashes. 'I know why you did it—because I saved his life that night. But, Rod, and this is what I really came to say, it's enough for me just to see him fit and well. You didn't have to do that. And anyway, when our divorce comes through and you marry Marianne, well then. . . .'

She found she couldn't continue, but sat staring at her hands in an agony of embarrassment as the silence lengthened.

Rod said finally, 'Why did you go to see him last night, Bobbie?'

'I've never . . . seen him race before.'

He waited for her to continue, but she couldn't, and finally he pushed his chair back and walked over to the bureau where he pulled something from the drawer. He brought it over to her and put it down on the table in front of her.

'What's this?' she asked.

'Morningtown's assessment card. Have a look at it.' His voice was even.

Bobbie unfolded the card and he leant forward and plucked it from her fingers and turned it over.

'Read the change of ownership entry.'

She did as she was bid, noting the official Trotting Board stamp next to the entry that signified that Morningtown was now raced by Mr and Mrs R. Simpson. And in the act of glancing up at his set face, she paused and stared. For the date on the stamp was at least a fortnight before the horse's attack of colic.

'I ... I don't understand,' she stammered.

Rod sat down again and surveyed her bleakly before he said, 'It's quite simple really. Viv came to me, the day before her wedding as a matter of fact, and told me that she and Richard planned to buy a block of land and build a house in Perth. She asked me if I'd like to buy her share in the horse so she'd be able to contribute towards it. I offered to lend her the money instead, but she was quite adamant—you know how Viv is——' he smiled briefly, 'so I agreed. And then, when *you* agreed to marry me, I decided it would make a good wedding present for you. But unfortunately I didn't get the transfer through in time, so I decided to keep it as a surprise for the first time he raced—in our joint names. Which was last night.'

The silence lengthened. Bobbie found herself quite unable to comprehend what this meant and she started to speak several times, but the words wouldn't come. She shot Rod an anxious look, to see he was sprawled back in his chair, and took fright again at the look in his narrowed grey eyes.

And when he finally broke the tense silence it was to say quietly but with an underlying note of steel in his voice, 'Bobbie, I'm not letting you out of here until we clear up something else. And it's this. How come you're so certain that I'm passionately in love with Marianne? That despite being thirty-one, I could make a school-boy blunder and marry the wrong girl? Just how did you arrive at this conclusion? And don't bother to lie to me, Bobbie, because that will only make me angrier.'

She licked her lips and stared down at her hands. But as usual, the power of his personality was too strong for her and she found herself forced to meet his eyes.

'She . . . told me,' she said finally.

'When?' He shot at her.

'The . . . the day we were married. She came to see me. She said—you'd had a row and you were only marrying me in a fit of pique. She said. . . .' She looked at him helplessly.

'Go on,' he commanded harshly.

'She said that you wouldn't be able to stay away from her for long. That. . . .' She shrugged her shoulders helplessly. 'That . . . I was too immature and un-sophisticated for you.'

'And you believed her,' he said flatly.

'I . . . she had proof!' Bobbie said desperately.

'What kind of proof?'

'Some photos of you and—and the fact that you took her to dinner the night before our wedding. And . . . that night, when she rang up, she said she was going away with you and . . . and *even* the day before yester-day there was a picture in the paper of her . . . with Morningtown.' Her voice quivered.

Rod sat forward and said intently, 'Was that why you ran away from Tracey?'

'Yes,' she whispered, and felt the tears spill over and trickle down her cheeks. 'You see, you didn't come. Not once.'

'Bobbie,' he said roughly, and pulled an impatient hand through his hair, 'did it never occur to you that she was lying?'

'She had proof, Rod!'

'Bobbie, I don't know what photos she showed you, but I can tell you quite categorically that it's at least twelve months since I've been photographed anywhere with Marianne, and as a matter of fact that one of her with Morningtown is even older than that. It was taken not long after I met her and the occasion was when Morningtown won the four-year-old championship.'

'But . . . but you took her to dinner the night before our wedding—and the night before that—she said.'

'That's not quite correct,' he said tautly. 'She arrived on this doorstep uninvited on both occasions. The first night was to verify what Mike Findlay of all people had told her that we were getting married. When I confirmed it—and believe me, Bobbie, she had no cause to have any expectations in that regard herself, because despite an initial attraction which I will never deny, it wasn't long before I discovered that Marianne was probably the most self-centred person I'd ever met—when I confirmed it she acted quite normally, and as I was eating myself and probably because I felt slightly guilty about not telling her sooner, I offered her something to eat.'

'And . . . and the next night?'

'The next night,' he said broodingly, 'was somewhat different. She arrived in a state of hysteria almost and flung herself on me and threatened to do away with herself if I went through with this marriage.' He stared at the table before lifting his eyes and saying quietly, 'Bobbie, in any other circumstances I would have never told anyone this, but perhaps I should have told *you* sooner. Marianne is—how can I put it— perhaps chronically neurotic is the right term. I didn't realise it myself for some time, but when I did, I went to see her father and he confirmed it. The attachment she claimed to profess for me was identical to what she had gone through with countless men. I'm not quite sure what first alerted me. I think it was that if you know her long enough you can't help but realise that she's basically— irrational.'

Bobbie couldn't help shivering suddenly at the bleak look in his eyes.

He went on, 'It's very hard to—simply abandon someone who you know is not quite responsible for their actions. I'm not saying she's mental or insane, but she is subject to bouts of nervous tension that seem to . . . to be able to swallow any powers of logic she might possess. I know that not six months ago she went through this same trauma with someone else, someone I knew very well. I think perhaps and I hope with all my heart that this will happen, that she will meet some man some day who is equal to the task. I know I never could be, but I realised some time before I found out the rest that I didn't want to be. And I had thought that I'd achieved her recognition of this fact. It seems I had not, but all I can say is that any dealings I've had with her for a long time now have been purely in the spirit of someone who is aware of her problems. You see, I can't but help share the fear that her father has, that one day she'll fall into some . . . unscrupulous hands.'

'I'm so sorry,' Bobbie said through her tears. 'But you see I didn't know. And when you suggested a marriage of convenience, when you said you wanted to marry someone suitable and not necessarily wildly in love with you—well, it all seemed to fall into place.'

Rod made an abrupt movement and said, 'Those words were possibly ill-chosen.'

'What do you mean?' she whispered, and added in agonised tones, 'That's the trouble, you see. I must be too immature for you, because half the time, I don't . . . know what you mean.'

He stared at her and sighed deeply.

She went on, 'When you didn't come to see me, when

you were so anxious to have me go and stay with Tracey. . . .'

He said very gently, 'Did you want me to come, Bobbie?'

She closed her eyes and said huskily, 'I didn't want to go!' And though, There, it's out now. He must realise.

She opened her eyes at a sound and found him standing beside her.

'Put your coat on, Bobbie. We're going for a walk.'

'. . . .All right.' She stood up dazedly and he took her arm.

They walked side by side in silence through the golden afternoon and Bobbie realised Rod was leading her up the hill to the big tree. A gentle breeze was brushing the long grass now with a soft sighing sound and she breathed in deeply.

'Bobbie,' he said at last, 'I'm going to tell you a curious story. And when I've told you, you can make your decision for once and for all. It's about a man who thought himself, to use your phrase, the epitome of maturity and sophistication. Who had come to a time in his life when he found himself feeling rather—cynical, I suppose, and disillusioned. He had had one very deeply felt love affair in his younger days that hadn't ended happily, and although it hadn't rankled for a long time, it had perhaps contributed to this feeling of disillusionment.'

Tracey, she thought stupidly. Is he talking about himself and Tracey?

They walked with Bluey trotting along obediently behind them.

Rod went on, 'And then one day, not so long ago, he met a girl who was very young and unversed in the ways of the world and he found to—I must admit—to his astonishment, that he was falling head over heels in love with her. And he went to great, I suppose some people would say ridiculous lengths, to make sure that this girl didn't slip through his fingers. Because he knew that crazy as it seemed, he couldn't contemplate the thought of that.'

Bobbie walked steadily enough beside him, but her heart was anything but steady, and she wondered if she was drunk on the golden, scented afternoon air and her ears were deceiving her.

Rod's voice was deep and even as he said, 'But he never got any real indication that this girl returned his feelings, and he had a terrible fear of two things. One was that she had never had the opportunity to experiment with her emotions as most girls of her age have and therefore wouldn't be willing to tie herself down so young and with someone quite a bit older than she was. And as his passion seemed to grow almost daily, his second fear was that in her youth and inexperience she could feel frightened by the intensity of what he felt for her.'

He didn't look at her as he continued, 'So he resolved to woo her very gently. Unfortunately circumstances intervened and in something akin to panic he . . . made his move rather earlier than he had planned, and in doing so, and with these two fears very prominent in his mind, he said and did some things that he regrets even now. And once they were married it seemed to him as if his fears had been well grounded, because apart from one fleeting occasion she still gave him no indication that she returned any part of his . . . love.'

Bobbie found she was breathing rapidly, and it wasn't due to the fact that they were climbing steadily now.

Rod went on, 'And that one fleeting occasion could

unfortunately be interpreted as the natural response of a young girl approaching womanhood. No more, no less. But despite this he found himself falling deeper and deeper in love with her, not only for her beauty but her pluck and spirit, in fact everything about her. And it got to the stage that he found he could no longer trust himself with her. He wanted to be assured that she was content to be his for the rest of her life and he wanted her desperately in his bed.'

Bobbie made an inarticulate sound.

'But one day, some measure of sanity returned to him and he realised that he couldn't continue what was fast becoming an experiment in torture for him, while he watched this young girl becoming as unhappy as he was. So he decided on a period of separation, hoping against desperate hope that this would allow her to make a free, unforced decision to return to him. They proved to be the longest and hardest days of his life, but he's still . . . resolved to stand by that decision. There will be no more coercion.'

As he spoke those last words they gained the summit of the hill and stood looking around, and Bobbie found her heart pounding as she realised he had no more to say. He was standing a few paces from her, half turned away, but she could see the lines etched in his face as she had seen last night.

Then something seemed to snap inside her, the last barrier, and she heard herself say, 'Rod, can I tell *you* a story?'

He closed his eyes briefly and turned towards her.

'It's about a very young, inexperienced girl who met a man she thought she detested. But it wasn't very long before she found herself prey to the craziest, incredible dreams and sensations. But because it had never happened to her before, because she couldn't believe that a man like this could possibly love someone so young and naïve, so . . . unwordly, who he'd mistaken for a boy in the first place, she decided to bury those . . . dreams. To put them down as an adolescent crush which would surely wane.'

Rod made no movement. It was as if he was afraid to move or speak.

Bobbie said, 'But this girl found that, if anything, what she felt grew stronger, and finally she knew that all she wanted from life was to be allowed to share his bed and his life and bear his children.'

Her voice grew husky, but she went on steadily, 'Which was what she intended to do, on any basis and even though she thought he didn't love her. That is, until . . . certain circumstances intervened which in her youth and silliness she attached more importance to than she should have. But she found that even while she did this, she was still hopelessly, desperately in love with this man. And there were many, many days while they were together that she wanted above all to reveal how she felt.'

She smiled wryly as she said, 'You see, she had a terrible fear too. That this great burgeoning of feeling she was—still is—experiencing, would only seem childish and perhaps—amusing to someone as worldly as this man, and finally only become a burden to him.'

Still he made no movement and it was Bobbie who took the final step. She said simply, 'Rod, take me now, please.'

Then she was in his arms being kissed until the view swam before her eyes and she found she couldn't stand without his supporting arm and he was murmuring her name over and over again.

And the wind rustled the dry leaves of the great tree that stood sentinel beside them.

Mills & Boon
Best Seller Romances

The very best of Mills & Boon Romances
brought back for those of you who missed
them when they were first published.

In July
we bring back the following four
great romantic titles.

FIRE AND ICE
by Janet Dailey

To fulfil the terms of her mother's will Alisa had to be married
before she was allowed to look after her young half-sister, and
Zachary Stuart was the only man prepared to marry her. But
Alisa's idea of marriage differed very much from that of her
new husband!

THE IMPOSSIBLE MARRIAGE
by Lilian Peake

Old Mrs. Dunlop thought it was a splendid idea to leave her
large house and a lot of money to her great-nephew Grant Gard
and her young friend Beverley Redmund — on condition that
within six months they got married. There was one snag: the
two people concerned just couldn't stand each other!

WIND RIVER
by Margaret Way

Perri had come here to Coorain, in the Dead Heart of
Australia, to work, not to teeter on the brink of disaster with a
man like the cattle baron Gray Faulkner. But how could she avoid
it?

THE GIRL AT GOLDENHAWK
by Violet Winspear

Jaine was used to taking back place to her glamorous cousin
Laraine, and as it seemed only natural to Laraine and her mother
that Jaine should take on the difficult task of explaining to her
cousin's wealthy suitor that she had changed her mind about the
marriage, Jaine nerved herself to meet the arrogant Duque Pedro
de Ros Zanto. But there was a surprise in store . . .

If you have difficulty in obtaining any of these books through
your local paperback retailer, write to:

Mills & Boon Reader Service
P.O. Box 236, Thornton Road, Croydon, Surrey, CR9 3RU.

From this month three great Doctor Nurse Romances

From July on, Mills & Boon publish an extra title
in this very popular collection. Each month, there
are three for you to look out for and enjoy. These
are the titles for July

ALL FOR CAROLINE
by Sarah Franklin

Megan Lacey takes up the job of speech therapist simply
as a way of avenging her cousin's broken heart. But she
makes a complete mess of things — and loses her own
heart into the bargain.

THE SISTER AND THE SURGEON
by Lynne Collins

Sister Ruth Challis is amazed to find her cold heart
melting towards untrustworthy consultant, Oliver Manning,
but complications increase when her old friend Daniel's
feelings about her become significant . . .

SOUTH ISLAND NURSE
by Belinda Dell

When both the Senior Medical Registrar, Sandy Legrady,
and the new house physician, Ian Dugall, vie for her
attention, Staff Nurse Erica Ryall is forced to juggle with
their affections . . .

On sale where you buy Mills & Boon romances.

The Mills & Boon rose is the rose of romance

The Mills & Boon Rose is the Rose of Romance

Every month there are ten new titles to choose from — ten new
stories about people falling in love, people you want to read
about, people in exciting, far-away places. Choose Mills & Boon.
It's your way of relaxing:

July's titles are:

SUMMER FIRE *by Sally Wentworth*
Why had Pandora ensured that the haughty but charming Sir
James Arbory would never look at her twice?

CASTLES OF SAND *by Anne Mather*
Little Hussein was Ashley's son, but she must never let him know
who she was. How could she put up with the hostility of
Hussein's formidable uncle Alain . . .

SPITFIRE *by Lindsay Armstrong*
Rod Simpson had bought Bobbie's home and let her stay there.
But what happened when his sister got married and went away?

STRANGERS INTO LOVERS *by Lilian Peake*
There was nothing between Gillian Taylor and Randall West
any more, except two people, one who loved Gillian and another
who loved Randall. And of course, Gary . . .

ABDUCTION *by Charlotte Lamb*
The worst thing that had happened to Marisa was for her baby
to be snatched. It also brought her estranged husband Gabriel
back on the scene . . .

ONE OF THE BOYS *by Janet Dailey*
Petra Wallis fell in love with her boss, the dominating Dane
Kingston. But he had no more use for her as a woman than as
a technician . . .

THE FLAME OF DESIRE *by Carole Mortimer*
Sophie's marriage to Luke Vittorio was a mockery. She had the
best of reasons for knowing he was still having an affair with
her stepmother . . .

THE SAVAGE TOUCH *by Helen Bianchin*
Lee was very much attracted to Marc Leone. But nothing was
going to deflect her from her real goal in life: to marry a
millionaire!

MIXED FEELINGS *by Kerry Allyne*
Kylie's boss, Grant Brandon, was old enough to be her father.
So there was no need for his disagreeable nephew, Race Brandon,
to be so scathing about her!

A TASTE OF PARADISE *by Margaret Mayo*
Her fiancé had not told Cathy about the unyielding Grant Howard,
who lived on the island she had received as a wedding present . . .

If you have difficulty in obtaining any of these books from your
local paperback retailer, write to:

Mills & Boon Reader Service
P.O. Box 236, Thornton Road, Croydon, Surrey, CR9 3RU.